D1626710

The Lady Grace Mysteries

www.kidsatrandomhouse.co.uk

Also available

The Lady Grace Mysteries

HAUNTED

Grace Cavendish

Jan Burchett and Sara Vogler are writing as Grace Cavendish

DOUBLEDAY
London • New York • Toronto • Sydney • Auckland

THE LADY GRACE MYSTERIES: HAUNTED
A DOUBLEDAY BOOK 978 0 385 60853 4 (from January 2007)
0 385 60853 5

Published in Great Britain by Doubleday,
an imprint of Random House Children's Books

This edition published 2006

1 3 5 7 9 10 8 6 4 2

Series created by Working Partners Ltd
Copyright © Working Partners Ltd, 2006
Cover illustration by David Wyatt

Papers used by Random House Children's Books are natural, recyclable products
made from wood grown in sustainable forests. The manufacturing processes
conform to the environmental regulations of the country of origin.

Typeset in Bembo by Palimpsest Book Production Limited,
Polmont, Stirlingshire

RANDOM HOUSE CHILDREN'S BOOKS
61–63 Uxbridge Road, London W5 5SA
A division of The Random House Group Ltd

RANDOM HOUSE AUSTRALIA (PTY) LTD
20 Alfred Street, Milsons Point, Sydney,
New South Wales 2061, Australia

RANDOM HOUSE NEW ZEALAND LTD
18 Poland Road, Glenfield, Auckland 10, New Zealand

RANDOM HOUSE (PTY) LTD
Isle of Houghton, Corner of Boundary Road & Carse O'Gowrie,
Houghton 2198, South Africa

THE RANDOM HOUSE GROUP Limited Reg. No. 954009
www.**kids**at**randomhouse**.co.uk

A CIP catalogue record for this book is available from the British Library.

Printed and bound by
Clays Ltd, St Ives plc

For Mirka Tepsa with lots of love

Most Privy and Secrete

The daybooke of my Lady Grace
Cavendish, Maid of Honour to
Her Glorious Majesty
Queen Elizabeth I of that name

At Medenham Manor, Wiltshire,
England

Evil Be to Any Who Look Herein

In my bedchamber

It is nine of the clock and it is our first morning at Medenham Manor. We are on summer progress with Her Majesty and the Court.

I am almost ready to attend the Queen, wearing a gown of carnation red, slashed all over with lozenge shapes to show the pink lining underneath. It was one of the Queen's and she gave it to me just before we came away. Now that it has been altered it fits very well, for I am almost as tall as Her Majesty, although I am skinnier.

I have dressed myself and the only thing I cannot do is tie on my sleeves. But everyone is too busy to help. They are fussing round Lady Sarah Bartelmy, who has suddenly insisted that she wants her new string of seed pearls stitched round her bodice, just as the Queen has. Olwen, Lady Sarah's tiring woman, is struggling with the task because she will not stand still. Fran is trying to help Mary Shelton dress while Mary is trying to do Sarah's hair! It is Bedlam here, and quite comical to watch them all flapping about like chickens!

Of course, I would be ready if I had a tiring woman of my own instead of having to share Fran with Mary. Sometimes it is quite hard being the youngest Maid of Honour.

I have taken refuge on my bed with my new daybooke. It is a beautiful book with a cover of finest blue vellum and was given to me by a dear friend. I will take this time to record our arrival at Medenham Manor.

A few minutes later

I broke off just now to watch the fun. Poor Olwen is having a terrible time with her sewing. It is taking such an age — I could certainly not be bothered with it.

'Please could you stand still, my lady?' pleaded Olwen. 'My needle has come unthreaded again.'

'I have been standing still for more than an hour!' snapped Lady Sarah.

I felt like piping up that my peevish lady had not stood still at all, but I did not want anything thrown at me, so I kept quiet.

'Why do you not wear your green gown?' suggested Mary Shelton calmly, as she combed Lady Sarah's hair. 'It is very becoming and needs no ornament.'

'What!' exclaimed Lady Sarah. 'Last year's fashion? Have you lost your wits, Mary?'

It was brave of Mary to suggest this. She should have known that the ancient green gown (three months old) had been packed merely for extreme emergencies.

But I will block my ears to it all and write about Medenham Manor instead. This is the most modern house I have ever been in. Indeed, it is so new that it is not quite finished, and everywhere smells of paint and plaster and new wood. Our host, Lord Reynold

Waldegrave, the fifth Earl of Medenham, decided last year that the whole of his old house needed renovating. So he started knocking bits down and then rebuilding them in the latest style.

We are in the new west wing. Mary Shelton, Lady Sarah and I share a lovely chamber with a dressing room beyond. Our trunks are stowed in there. (The trunks are luckier than some members of the Court who needs must stay in the village. This often happens on progress. Few of the fine houses at which we stay are big enough to afford all of us chambers.) Our room is very spacious but Lady Sarah can make anywhere seem crowded.

I wonder where my good friends Masou and Ellie are. Mr Somers always makes sure that Masou and the rest of the Queen's tumbling troupe are comfortable, but poor Ellie will probably have to sleep on some floor or other. Being a mere laundrymaid, she never gets a bed or even a palliasse. But there is nothing I can do about it for I am not supposed to be friends with her – or with Masou – at all. It is not thought seemly for a Maid of Honour. I think the Queen knows that I am friends with them but she pretends she does not so that she won't have to stop me.

We are to accompany the Queen to church soon – if we are ever ready! Lord Reynold has arranged a special service to give thanks for Her Majesty's safe arrival. After that we are to have a tour of this splendid house. At least, Lord Reynold has told us that his manor is splendid. We arrived here last night and it was too late to see for ourselves. Our journey was delayed by a sudden summer storm, so there was only time for supper and then bed. Lord Robert Dudley, the Earl of Leicester, did nothing but grumble at the supper table.

'My Liege,' I heard him complaining in a low voice to the Queen, 'do you truly need to bide here for a whole week? My home at Kenilworth is ready for you and I fear this storm presages some evil.'

'Fie, Robert!' snapped the Queen, waving a chicken leg at him. 'We will be at Kenilworth anon. I have promised Lord Reynold I will stay here and I look forward to it. As for evil, 'tis nothing but some drops of rain and rumbles of thunder!'

The Earl of Leicester always wants the Queen to himself. It is said he is in love with her, and he is indeed her favourite, but she does not like to have her actions questioned. Secretly, though, I wanted the Queen to take Lord Robert's advice. Not because of bad omens, but because the entertainments at Kenilworth are always marvellous, while I have the feeling that it is going to be boring staying here for a whole week!

Anyhow, this morning we are to go to church and then this afternoon we are to have the grand tour. Lord Reynold is desperate for the Queen to see the changes to his manor. He almost melted with joy when Her Majesty arrived and the royal feet actually stepped onto his flagstones!

Heavens be praised! I think Fran has finished dressing Mary! It must be my turn at last.

About ten minutes later

I am still not dressed, but no matter! I have something of great interest to record. Fran had just finished with Mary Shelton when the door to the bedchamber was flung open so suddenly that it nearly knocked her out of the window! Lady Jane Coningsby burst in with Carmina Willoughby close behind. The room felt even more crowded now that there were five Maids of Honour and two tiring women within.

'Girls,' breathed Jane, putting her hand dramatically over her heart, 'you will not believe what we have heard—'

'Then there is no point in telling us!' snapped Lady Sarah. Lady Jane is not Sarah's favourite person in the world and she was getting very impatient with Olwen's slow, careful stitching of the pearls, especially as Fran was now trying to help too.

'But we *must* tell you,' squeaked Carmina excitedly, 'else I shall burst!'

'That would be most unpleasant,' laughed Mary Shelton. 'You had better give us the story straight away.'

'Well,' whispered Carmina, drawing us around her, 'we overheard the two servants who brought us our water this morning—'

'It was *I* who was telling the tale,' Lady Jane interrupted crossly. 'It seems that this house has a dread secret. It is—'

'Haunted!' shrieked Carmina, looking terrified and tremendously excited at the same time. 'One hundred years ago the first Earl was murdered, and because he met his death so violently his ghost used to walk in this very house! And now it is said that, since the building work began, he has been seen again in the old east wing!'

Jane looked most put out at having her moment of glory stolen like that – but everyone else gasped and Lady Sarah turned quite pale. I have to confess I felt a flutter of excitement. I hope the story is true. I have never seen a ghost before.

'I have heard something of the first Earl,' said Mary Shelton. 'Lord Reynold told me that his ancestor made money selling arms. And this was at the time of the war between the Yorkists and the Lancastrians, so there was a great demand for weapons and armour. The Earl did very well.'

''Tis a pity he did not keep some armour for himself,' I couldn't help saying, 'for then he might not have been murdered!'

'Lord Reynold did not mention a murder,' said Mary, picking through her box of gloves. 'But it is true that the first Earl did not stay long at Medenham Manor.'

'So what happened to him then if he wasn't done to death?' demanded Carmina, who obviously didn't want her ghost story to be spoiled.

'Lord Reynold said the first Earl ran away to Cornwall with his mistress,' replied Mary. 'His son took over his house and all his business.'

'Then there cannot be a ghost,' I said in disappointment, 'unless it travelled all the way back from Cornwall!'

But Carmina was not going to let the ghost

lie. 'This house must be haunted,' she insisted, 'for the Queen has heard of it!'

'Has she?' gasped Mary Shelton, forgetting all about her gloves.

'Yes,' said Carmina. 'She knew about it even before we started on progress.'

'I am surprised the Queen let us come here then,' sniffed Lady Sarah.

'Well, apparently the Queen threatened not to come,' Lady Jane put in, determined to have her say. 'But Lord Reynold assured her that the stories were mere tittle-tattle.'

'That is what I would say too' – I laughed – 'if I was hoping for a visit from Her Majesty. I would claim that all the tales were untrue and hope the ghost didn't appear while she was at my house.'

'But imagine the trouble if it did,' said Carmina, wide-eyed. 'The Queen would be furious. When they realized we had heard them, the servants begged us not to tell anyone. Her Majesty has forbidden any talk of ghosts, for she does not want her Court gibbering and twitching with fear at every turn.'

'I hope she did not include us!' retorted Lady Sarah, pulling away from Olwen and turning in front of the looking glass to inspect her pearls. 'I have never gibbered or twitched in my life, and I am not afraid of ghosts.'

'I am!' declared Carmina, peering anxiously around the room.

'You heard a great deal from those two servants,' I said curiously – I confess I was impressed with their spying!

'They thought us asleep' – Carmina giggled – 'and we kept our heads under our covers so we would hear all.'

'Servants are such gossipmongers!' said Lady Jane scornfully.

I wanted to laugh. Lady Jane had not wasted a moment in passing the gossip on to us!

I wish we did not have to go to church this morning. It is not that I am irreverent. I am just eager for the tour to start, especially as there may be a ghost about! I think I shall try to stay at the back of the party and hope for a visitation. How silly of me to think that when we arrived here at Medenham Manor,

I would be bored. It seems there is a ghost to be found! And who better to search for it than Grace Cavendish, secret Lady Pursuivant to Her Majesty. None of the Court knows that the Queen has appointed me to seek out all those who would trouble her peace. And if a ghost wouldn't trouble her peace, I don't know what would! There is only one problem: I do not think Her Majesty would want me to go ghost hunting. Still, if I do not tell her anything about it, I will only be following her own orders that we are not to speak of the ghost!

Mary Shelton says that her groom does not believe in ghosts. I thought that strange, for surely everyone knows that sometimes a dead soul cannot rest and so returns to haunt the living. I have never heard tell of someone who did not *believe* in ghosts before. Mayhap he will see the ghost while we are staying at Medenham Manor and so will change his mind!

Hell's teeth! I can hear the bells calling us to the service and I have still not got my sleeves on!

In the Great Hall

There is more to this ghost story!

It is near two of the clock and we have returned from church. We are having dinner in the Great Hall before the promised tour, and I am trying to write and eat at the same time. I have my daybooke on my lap, where I am sure to get the pages stained if I am not careful, but I want to record the events of this morning.

As soon as we heard the church bells chime for the service everyone started rushing about finding hats and gloves, though I was still sleeveless and Carmina was still chattering on about the ghost.

'Do you think it drips blood?' she gasped. 'Or carries its head under its arm?'

Suddenly Mrs Champernowne, the Mistress of the Maids, appeared in our chamber. Carmina stopped talking immediately and looked at her feet.

But Mrs Champernowne has sharp ears. 'Have you been gossiping, girls?' She frowned, folding her arms across her large bosom. 'There is nothing to be gained from any silly tittle-tattle, especially if it is about ghosts and the like. Her Majesty will be most displeased. She has forbidden all talk of phantoms and rightly so. Speaking of such things will surely bring evil on you all.' Then she spotted my lack of sleeves. 'Look at you, Grace!' she said. 'Not ready and you have surely had long enough!'

I tried to tell her that it wasn't my fault, that Lady Sarah's pearls had needed the attention of both our tiring women, but she would hear none of it and ordered Fran to deal with me straight away. Poor Fran had hardly tied the last ribbon when Mrs Champernowne bustled us out to attend the Queen.

St Augustine's Church is close to the manor house and we followed Her Majesty and Lord Reynold in a great procession to its door. I had hoped to get a good look at the east wing as we went, but Mrs Champernowne chivvied us along and I did not dare linger.

Her Majesty wore a gown of white satin in the Spanish style, with hanging sleeves and a beautiful high ruff. Round her neck she had a carcanet of gold links set with diamonds and rubies. It was hard to believe that she had travelled a full twelve miles yesterday! She looked magnificent.

As we walked, Lord Reynold pointed out any interesting feature of his new building and grounds that we could see from the church path – mostly features that he has designed himself and of which he is therefore very proud. But that makes him sound like a boastful man, which he is not. He is just like a little boy – although bigger and rounder and with a redder face – for he is enthusiastic about everything. Everybody likes him, and it is well known that the Queen thinks highly of him.

We were nearing the church when Her Majesty beckoned to me. 'I thought my eyes were deceiving me,' she said sternly as I approached. 'However, I see that you are indeed Lady Grace Cavendish. For a moment I thought a vagabond had taken your place.'

I had no idea what the Queen was talking about.

'Do not look so puzzled, Grace,' she told me. 'Just make sure that you are completely dressed in future before you wait on me. Now, pray attend to those sleeve laces!'

I looked down at my sleeves. Fran's hasty bows had come undone and the sleeves were gaping open at the tops and showing my chemise beneath.

'I beg Your Majesty's pardon,' I said hastily, trying to pull the sleeves closed while making a deep curtsy at the same time. 'We have but two tiring women for the three of us, and some of us need more help than others.' Then I realized that I sounded as if I were moaning. 'I would not for the world complain,' I hurried on, 'and were I a spider and blessed with extra arms I should be able to do my own lacing.'

Her Majesty roared with laughter. 'An eight-legged Maid of Honour!' she guffawed. 'That would be a sight to see. I should have you in Mr Somers's troupe spinning webs to entertain us all.' She beckoned to the Mistress of the Maids. 'Mrs Champernowne,' she said, 'please look to Lady Grace's sleeves – and count yourself lucky that she has only two arms!'

Mrs Champernowne's face was a picture. She obviously had no idea what Her Majesty was talking about! It can be hard to keep up with Her Majesty's mood changes. But she is my favourite person in the whole world and the best godmother I could ever have. Of course I wish my own mother had not died saving the Queen's life, but since I cannot change that, I am glad that Her Majesty chose to keep me with her at Court.

Mrs Champernowne huffed and puffed with my sleeves but she didn't dare tell me off. Then we had to hurry to catch up with the others, and her face was quite red by that time!

When we reached the church, we saw that it was very small. I am sure that Lord Reynold would have knocked it down and built a bigger one in its place if he'd had the time. Most of the Court had to stay outside and kick their heels in the churchyard. Mayhap they had the better deal, for the service was extremely long.

The poor village priest, Master Peabody, was quite overcome with the grand company that filled his church, and his nerves made him gabble. I thought he would never finish mumbling his thanks to the Lord for our safe journey, for the fine weather today, for the blessed bell ringers, and most of all for the presence of Her Most Gracious Majesty who deigned to smile on us all. I noticed that the Queen was not smiling after an age of such discourse!

I was glad to get back out into the summer sunshine at last. But we were not to go back to Medenham Manor straight away. As soon as the Queen had led the congregation outside she was persuaded back in by Lord Reynold so that he could point out the fine rose window, which he had commissioned at the time of her coronation. He had obviously waited eleven years to show it to her and was not going to miss this chance. I wonder how many more windows he will be presenting for her inspection!

'I would be delighted, my lord,' said the Queen graciously. Her Majesty is always delighted to see something that has been done specially in her honour. The Ladies-in-Waiting attended her, but we Maids were allowed to wait outside, thank Heaven.

'I wonder where the tomb of the first Earl is,' I said.

'Do you mean the one who is supposed to be the ghost?' gasped Carmina, her eyes darting eagerly about. 'Quick, let us look!'

'Surely the Waldegraves have a grand tomb inside the church,' said Lady Sarah. 'Although I confess I did not see one.'

'Lord Reynold told me that his ancestors considered the church too small to house a fitting tomb for their family,' Mary Shelton told us. 'The entrance to their vault is somewhere in the churchyard.'

We walked sedately among the graves, glancing at the inscriptions as we went. At last we turned a corner and came upon a part of the graveyard that was separated by a low hedge of rosemary. There was no doubt that this was where the Waldegraves were laid to rest, for here was a large vault with plaques on its walls and yew trees growing around it.

'Some say that ghosts return to the place of their burial,' whispered Carmina. 'Do you think we will see the spectre here?'

We peered at the plaques and found the names of the second, third and fourth earls, but there was nothing for the first.

'Good day, my ladies,' came a sudden gruff voice from behind us.

We all jumped and Lady Sarah let out a squeal!

A grizzled old man was walking along the path towards us, his battered hat in his hand. He was certainly no ghost! 'Are you looking for anything in particular?' he asked. 'We have some fine stones in this place, and I should know, for I've been gravedigger here, man and boy, for forty years.' He grinned horribly, showing toothless gums.

Lady Sarah pushed me forwards.

'Er, I . . . that is, we . . .' I stammered. I was not scared, but the stranger had come upon us rather unexpectedly. 'We are looking for the burial place of the first Earl of Medenham. Can you show us where it is, good sir?'

The old man's eyes widened and he came closer. This was unfortunate as he was rather smelly. 'Ben Boggis at your service,' he wheezed, touching his forelock – or the place where one would have been if he had had any hair. 'There's no monument for the old Earl and no coffin lyin' in yonder vault,' he told us. 'There never has been. My family has dug and tended graves here for centuries so I know it to be true.' He looked round furtively, and then added, 'And there's no grave because there was no body to put in it!'

So was there nothing to investigate after all? I wondered. Had the first Earl really run off with his mistress and died in distant Cornwall?

But the gravedigger hadn't finished. 'There are many stories about how the first Earl met his end,' he went on.

'Do tell us!' breathed Carmina, with a shiver.

'Indeed, my lady, I will,' Ben Boggis replied. 'Some say as it were by the hand of his neigh-bour, Sir William Fawley. They were great rivals in the armoury business and Medenham arms always sold better. 'Tis said Sir William accused the Earl of spreading rumours that his weapons were poorly made. By all accounts the Earl were an honest man and had done no such thing, but he invited Sir William up to the manor to settle their differences over a good meal and a goblet o' mead. His lordship had no notion o' what was goin' to happen next!' The gravedigger paused to see how his words were working on us. I suppose he did not often get such an audience and he was making the most of it.

'On with your tale, man,' urged Lady Jane impatiently.

'Very good, your ladyship.' The old man gave a small bow and carried on. 'It is said that they dined in a room in the east wing. It's there still.'

'Which room is it?' asked Carmina.

'It's in the old part of the manor,' answered the gravedigger, 'and has not yet been pulled down. If you go around the house to the side of the east wing and look across the moat you're sure to see it. First you must look for the oriel window that sticks out on the ground floor. 'Tis the only one of its kind there and—'

'Does that window look into the room?' interrupted Carmina, who was leaning forward eagerly.

'No,' said Ben Boggis, shaking his head slowly. 'But the top of the oriel window is flat, and round the edge of that little roof you will see a low wall, shaped like the battlements of a castle. Now, mark it well, for behind that ledge, on the first floor—'

'Is the room where they dined?' I burst in.

'Aye, my lady, the very same,' the old man confirmed. 'After they had eaten, 'tis said the Earl made a toast to friendship, but Sir William would have none of it. He dashed his cup to the ground and drew his sword. The two men fought right bitterly until Sir William thrust his blade into the Earl's heart.' Ben Boggis paused at this to give us all time to gasp in horror. Then he nodded approvingly and carried on. 'Sir William dragged the body out onto that ledge, heaved it over the wall and cast it down into the moat. The water bore the body away to the river and it were never seen again. And they say the Earl's spirit walks the east wing and appears on that ledge, wailing and crying, "If thou be Fawley I shall fight thee to the death!"'

'Is that true?' gasped Mary Shelton.

'It's just one of the stories, my lady,' the gravedigger told us. 'There is another. You see, there were those at the time as said the old Earl had done a terrible thing that filled him with guilt and gnawed away at his very soul.'

'What was it?' asked Lady Sarah. Despite the fact that Ben Boggis is not young or handsome, she and Lady Jane were hanging on his every word, but I was beginning to think that the gravedigger was just a yarn spinner.

'According to this story,' said the old man, 'a poor beggar ran up to the Earl, one day when he were out riding, and demanded speech with him. The Earl told him to be gone, for he feared the beggar might have the plague – he looked so pale and ill. Later the poor man was discovered dead in the snow on the edge of the Earl's land. Sealed documents were found on the body bearing the Earl's name, so they were taken straight to him. To the Earl's horror, he read that the beggar was his own son, born out of wedlock to a serving wench! Thus the Earl learned that he had driven his own kith and kin away to die. The knowledge drove him to madness and in the end he could bear it no more. He took himself to the room above the oriel window and leaped from that same ledge as I told you of.'

Carmina clasped her hands together so tightly that her knuckles turned white.

'The river bore the body away and it were never seen again,' said Ben Boggis. 'And they say the Earl's spirit walks the east wing and appears on that ledge, wailing and crying, "My son! My son!"'

'So which is the true story?' I asked impatiently.

'Neither,' chuckled the gravedigger. 'They're just tales told to frighten children.'

And Maids of Honour, I thought.

'So I suppose nobody knows the truth,' said Lady Jane, sounding disappointed.

The old man stared piercingly at each of us in turn, his eyes burning in his wrinkled old face. 'There's one here that does,' he whispered at last. 'And that's me.'

We all gaped at him as if he were a ghost himself.

'I had it from my father's own lips,' he told us, 'and he had it from his grandfather, so it's true. I know the rightful story of why the old Earl walks the east wing and shows himself on that ledge. He died a most horrible death and it happened this way—'

'Ladies!' came a familiar voice. We turned to see Mrs Champernowne bearing down on us from the church porch like an avenging fury. 'Hurry now! The Queen is waiting!' She stopped in her tracks when she saw who we were talking to. 'Come away immediately, girls,' she shrilled, flapping at us as if we were a flock of geese that had strayed. She glared disapprovingly at the gravedigger. 'I will thank you to let my Maids be,' she told him firmly as she pushed us away along the path.

How unlucky! Just as we were about to hear

the truth – or so Ben Boggis claimed – we were whisked away back to the manor! All the way, Mrs Champernowne ranted on about foolish Maids of Honour forgetting their station and talking with persons of a lower order, and smelly ones at that, and the other Maids muttered under their breath about the tales we had heard. And I made up my mind to come back and hear the real story of the ghost of the first Earl.

I must stop writing. Lord Reynold has just risen from his seat at the dinner table. I think he is going to give a speech.

A few moments later

Lord Reynold wanted to point out the twelve windows of the Great Hall and, what a surprise, they were made in honour of Her Gracious Majesty!

'One for each of the twelve glorious years

you have reigned over us,' he proclaimed as we raised our golden goblets. He hesitated and flushed a little. 'Well, at least, twelve years on the seventeenth day of November next.'

I saw his wife, Lady Celia, frown. And I wondered whether the original plan had been for the Queen to visit *next* summer – when the manor will be finished – and whether Lord Reynold's enthusiasm had landed Lady Celia with her royal visitor a year early!

The windows are most fine. There are six overlooking the main courtyard at the front and another six on the opposite wall, over-looking the Knot Garden at the back. They are all very modern, their many glass sections made in various jewel-like colours. The designs are most unusual, for each window shows a different weapon, all of which, I suppose, are made by the Medenham family. The entire Great Hall is beautifully panelled and carved with the family symbols and there is a musician's gallery at one end.

But now the Queen seems about to rise. It must be time for the tour of the house and grounds, so I will stop writing. I hope Lord Reynold has not finished with windows for today as there is one that interests me greatly: the oriel window with its ledge that featured in both the gravedigger's ghost stories.

The Great Hall – after the tour

It is just passed five of the clock and we are back in the Great Hall, where mead and sweetmeats have been laid out and a consort of recorders is warbling away in the gallery – not always in the same key! I have seen the Queen wince at least twice, but then she has a very fine musical ear. Lord Reynold is quick to tell us that the musicians are playing all the latest tunes. He is just like an eager young boy wanting to share his toys, and we all seem to become jollier in his company.

Now I will write of the tour. After dinner I had only just put away my daybooke when the Queen rose and we all hurried to our feet.

'Come, Lord Reynold,' she said, holding out her hand. 'I would see more of this splendid house about which I have heard so much.'

Lord Reynold shot to his feet, beaming all over his face. 'My Liege,' he breathed, bowing deeply, 'it would do me the greatest honour. My whole house is dedicated to Your Gracious Majesty. Indeed, the finished manor will be in the shape of a glorious letter E.' This was no surprise. Anyone who knows how to please Her Majesty builds a house in this shape. It is lucky that her name is not Clare or Beatrice, for curved manor houses would be hard to build! 'This hall is the upright of the E,' Lord Reynold explained, leading us towards a beau-tiful carved doorway, 'and the two wings and the porch in the middle, when it is built, will complete the letter. So with your leave I will show you the details of my new west wing.'

He took us in and out of many fine rooms and pointed out their best features in order to have the Queen's blessing on each and every one. I wished he had not installed so many vaulted ceilings, for I got a neck ache from looking up at them all! The last room in the west wing – and obviously Lord Reynold's pride and joy – was completely full of weapons and armour.

'I do hope you are not thinking of raising a rebellion against me, my lord!' exclaimed the Queen. 'For here there are enough arms for a whole army!'

I could see that Her Majesty had a twinkle in her eye as she spoke, but poor Lord Reynold was horrified.

'No indeed, My Liege,' he blustered, going pinker than ever and kneeling at her feet. 'I am your loyal servant. These are the weapons for the local Trained Bands – Medenham made, of course. As Lord Lieutenant of the County, I store them until your dutiful soldiers are called upon to fight.'

'I jest with you, man.' The Queen smiled, raising him to his feet. 'Come, show me those embossed shields.'

I groaned inwardly. There were so many of them. This was going to take hours! While they were talking, the rest of the Court took turns to squeeze into the chamber and admire the endless lines of swords, spears and axes. Lady Jane and Lady Sarah were in their element. The Earl's armoury was giving them the perfect opportunity to question the handsome young courtiers about the 'nasty weapons' and then lean on them for support when they were given gory answers. I was just beginning to wonder if we would ever get out when I suddenly felt as if someone was watching me from behind. I looked over my shoulder and gave a shriek!

Well, I think that it was most reasonable in the circumstances, though I am sorry that it gave alarm to all the people around me – especially Sir Pelham Poucher, who had to be taken away to recover with a glass of Madeira – but anyone would have shrieked at finding themselves staring up into an enormous visor!

Of course, I soon realized that the suit of armour it belonged to was empty, and I was not about to be hacked down where I stood, but it looked big enough for an elephant! And I want to state here and now that it was the sudden sight of it that made me yelp, and nothing to do with stories of the ghost of Medenham Manor.

By the time we left the room Lord Reynold was beaming more broadly than ever. I even heard him telling his secretary that 'in all future letters, no matter who the recipient be, mention is to be made of the Queen's praise in the first line'.

After the armoury, we were all led out into the main courtyard. On my left I could see the old east wing! Now I could have a good look at it. No work was going on while the Queen was staying so it stood silent and desolate. It was just the sort of place a ghost might like. I tried to spot the oriel window that the gravedigger had talked about, but then I remembered his words. I would have to go round to the outer wall of the east wing and look across the moat.

Lord Reynold was rubbing his hands together. 'I would not trouble Your Majesty with a tour of the rooms that remain of the east wing,' he said, 'for it is a blight on the symmetry of my manor, and would offend your eyes.' He then escorted the Queen across the main courtyard and over the ornate bridge that spanned the moat. I prayed that he would lead us to the left and round the outside of the east wing. But first we had to admire the wide-mouthed carp in the water, and then every rose in the garden beyond.

'You are but lacking a Tudor rose,' the Queen told Lord Reynold. 'I have in the gardens at Greenwich Palace a rose with white and red petals on the same flower. You must avail yourself of a cutting.'

For one awful moment I thought our host was going to set off there and then for London! But he contented himself with kneeling at the Queen's feet.

'Your Majesty is too kind,' he gasped, over-awed with the honour bestowed upon him. 'I would be delighted to have it growing here at Medenham.'

The Queen looked most pleased with this.

We walked on and I saw to my joy that the Rose Garden extended round to the outer side of the east wing – but Hell's teeth! Lord Reynold led us away from the house instead and up a slope towards a wood. Was I never going to see the ghost's window?

Now we had to admire the view of the manor from a distance!

'See the river Med yonder wending its way across Your Majesty's realm,' Lord Reynold declaimed, flinging out an arm. 'My ancestor had the foresight to divert a channel of the river around his house to form the moat. Thus it is never stagnant but flows gently back into the river from whence it came!'

I feared he was going to break into poetry that very moment! Fortunately, he did not. Though I suppose if it had been my house I would have been pleased with it too. The sun was sparkling on the water and the new parts of the manor were very stylish. The roof was adorned with lots of tall twisted chimneys and the current Earl's initials, RW, were worked into the stone balustrades.

I thought Lord Reynold's ancestor had been very clever with his moat. The river came out of a forest to our left and flowed away behind the house and off to the right. But a channel had been cut, bringing some of the water past the west wing, the front of the house and back round the old east wing, where it rejoined the river. And although the house was completely enclosed by water there were plenty of bridges across the moat.

Mary Shelton nudged me and pointed at the old part of the house. 'It is strange to think that one hundred years ago such funny buildings were considered so fine,' she said. 'Yet the first Earl must have been as pleased when he built it as Lord Reynold is with his renovations now.'

I was struck by Mary's words. This was interesting! I looked around to make sure that Mrs Champernowne was not in earshot. 'Are you saying that the ghost built the original Medenham Manor?' I asked.

'Yes, but of course he was not a ghost then,' giggled Mary. Then she lowered her voice as she remembered that the Queen had forbidden all talk of phantoms. ''Tis strange, for he did not linger long in his newly built home,' she whispered. 'I wonder what the true story is.'

At that moment an earnest-looking man bobbed up at Lord Reynold's elbow. I had seen him earlier on the tour trying to catch the Earl's attention.

Lord Reynold now turned to the Queen. 'My Liege,' he said, 'may I introduce to you my Master Builder, James Thompson.'

'Your work is very fine, Mr Thompson,' said the Queen graciously, as the earnest man bowed before her.

'Thank you, Your Majesty,' he gabbled nervously. 'I am humbly grateful to Lord Reynold for giving me this commission. An opportunity to work with such materials does not come often. If I may point out the stone carvings on the towers and the—'

'Thank you, Thompson,' Lord Reynold interrupted, briskly dismissing the builder and turning back to the Queen. 'With your permission, Your Majesty, we shall continue our tour and return to the Great Hall through the north door at the back. I wish to show you Lady Celia's Physic Garden on the way.'

Luck was certainly not on my side today, for Lord Reynold's route led us round the west of the house, as far away as we could possibly get from the east wing. So I have still not seen the ledge above the oriel window. I shall have to apply myself to the problem of how to sneak off and look at it for myself.

And now I can feel frowning eyes burning into me and they are from no ghost. Mrs Champernowne is looking in my direction. I will cease my writing and dutifully apply my ears to the recorders.

Very late – in my bedchamber

I am in my chamber with Lady Sarah and Mary Shelton. What an evening we have had! I must record it all in my daybooke. I have not yet managed to see the oriel window in the east wing, but I am even more determined to do so after what has happened! Lady Sarah is declaring that she will not sleep a wink and Mary Shelton, who is usually so calm and sensible, has agreed with her. For once, I will not be disturbing either of them with my candle – they are insisting that a light burn throughout the night.

After supper the Queen wished to discuss some business with Lord Reynold – probably something boring about weapons and foreign trade – so she made it clear that we were to amuse ourselves.

As it was still warm many of us walked out into the main courtyard. It was almost dark and although the moon was hidden behind clouds this evening, I could see that the Rose Garden on the far side of the moat was lit with torches. It was very fine and at another time I would have been enchanted by it, but tonight I just wanted to see the oriel window and its haunted ledge!

I kept an eye open for anyone who was heading round to the other side of the east wing, thinking that I would seize the opportunity to join them, for I could not be seen to wander the grounds unescorted. Mrs Champernowne's eagle eye would be sure to pick me out if I dared to behave in such an unseemly way!

Everyone made for the Rose Garden where many of the gentlemen took the opportunity to compare Lady Sarah with the lovely flowers. I will not repeat any of their poetic words for they made me feel sick enough the first time, but I was surprised to hear the redness of one rose being compared to the red of Lady Sarah's hair. They are quite different shades, but she seemed satisfied with the compliment and responded with much eyelash fluttering and bosom heaving. Lady Sarah is always popular with the young courtiers, and as the Queen was not there, she was the very centre of attention.

Of course, Lady Jane was jealous. She did have a fair number of young men hovering around her, but still she could not help casting envious glances at her rival from time to time.

Luckily, Lady Sarah's beauty was not the only topic of conversation. Because the Queen was absent, almost everyone was talking about spectres! Mary Shelton and I came upon a small group of Ladies-in-Waiting and gentlemen in an arbour entwined with honeysuckle. Carmina was sitting among them and she beckoned us over.

'Come quickly and hear Mr Bagshaw,' she squealed. 'He has been regaling us with terrifying stories of ghouls and ghosties.'

Mr Bagshaw is a jolly young man, but tonight he had sat himself beside one of the torches and the flickering light threw strange shadows across his face. It made him look eerie and mysterious.

'Enough of the spectral pig of Plymouth,' he was saying in a deep, solemn voice. 'On to the ghost of Medenham!'

Several people looked around in case the Queen had changed her mind and come into the gardens. But there was no sign of her. Her Majesty was still inside, no doubt dealing in daggers and pikes.

Mr Bagshaw leaned forward eagerly. 'I have heard that the ghost of Medenham had not been seen for a hundred years. But not long after Lord Reynold's builders moved the first brick of the old house, the spectre walked again! They say it haunts the old east wing.'

'Has Lord Reynold seen it?' breathed Carmina, clutching Mr Bagshaw's arm tightly.

'Who knows? He staunchly refuses to admit it exists!' said Mr Bagshaw, putting his hand over hers. 'He has threatened to dismiss any servant who speaks of it!'

'But whose ghost is it?' asked Lady Frances Clifford. 'And why does it walk at Medenham Manor?'

'We have heard some of the stories!' squeaked Carmina in excitement. 'Tell them, Grace.'

I had no option but to relate everything the gravedigger had told us earlier and in truth I enjoyed the telling. Everyone gazed at me in rapt attention, and I felt a little of the thrill that Masou says he gets from a good audience.

'So it is believed to be the first Earl,' I finished. 'But as to why he really walks, I do not know.'

I did not tell them where we had heard the tales, or that the gravedigger had been on the point of giving us the true story. It might have caused a headlong rush down to the graveyard!

Lady Frances shook herself. 'We must speak no more of Medenham Manor being haunted,' she said, looking a little pale, 'for the Queen will have us packed and away if she gets to hear of this. We have only just arrived. It would be very tedious to have the servants pack everything up again so soon.'

Mr Bagshaw got to his feet and bowed. 'I am ever your servant, Lady Frances, and will turn all conversation away from the unearthly visitations at Medenham Manor immediately.' He sat down again. 'Let me tell you instead of the ghost of Bradbury Village. But I warn you, it is a scary tale, for look, even the moon dares not show her face but hides behind the clouds in fright.'

Carmina huddled closer to the storyteller.

It was a wonderful story and Mr Bagshaw told it well. Everyone listened open-mouthed as he spoke of robbers and stabbings and foul murder. He had just got to the part where the villain was faced by the ghost of his victim.

'The murderer felt his blood freeze in his veins,' he told us dramatically. 'His heart began to pound until he thought it would burst out of his chest. The glowing phantom threw back his head and let out a terrible cry—'

And at that very moment a bloodcurdling scream pierced the night and sent shivers down my spine. Several of the gentlemen leaped up and put their hands to their swords.

Poor Mr Bagshaw was horror-struck. I am sure he had never had such a reaction to his tale before.

Almost immediately we saw Lady Jane rushing towards us, whimpering and clutching her skirts. 'A ghost!' she cried. And then, 'Save me!' she managed to whisper, before fainting dead away on the path. And it must have been a genuine faint for there was no handsome young man near enough to catch her!

Lady Frances ran to her side, followed by the rest of us.

Lady Jane stirred and opened her eyes. For

a moment she seemed bewildered and lost.

'What is the matter?' asked Lady Frances, helping her to sit up.

'I . . . I was walking with Lord Culpepper,' gulped Lady Jane. She was having trouble getting her words out and seemed genuinely scared! 'He wanted to show me a rose, a Maiden's Blush. He said that it had pretty pink petals like my cheeks . . .'

I was astonished. Even in her terror she had remembered the flirting!

'. . . but as we came to the place, and he bent down to a rose bush, I saw it.' Jane buried her face in her hands.

'What did you see?' I asked eagerly.

'Above the oriel window . . .' began Lady Jane.

'The window the gravedigger told us of?' whispered Mary. 'In the east wing?'

Lady Jane nodded weakly. 'It was standing there . . . on the ledge above.'

'What was?' demanded Carmina, giving her a little shake. 'What was standing there, Jane?'

'The ghost!' wailed Lady Jane.

A few minutes later

Zounds! I wish that Carmina and Lady Jane would learn to come into a bedchamber more quietly. They have just thrown the door open so violently that I swear the whole manor shook. Mary Shelton and Lady Sarah screamed, and that made Carmina and Jane scream back until I thought we would have the Gentlemen of the Guard along to sort us out! Finally they all calmed down.

'We are too scared to stay in our chamber,' Carmina told us breathlessly. 'I saw a shadow pass across the wall and our room is fully ten feet nearer the haunted east wing than this one, so any spectre is bound to come to us first!'

Now Lady Jane has got in with Mary Shelton and I am to share my bed with Carmina. There is barely room to move, let alone write.

Anyway, Lady Jane sat trembling in the Rose

Garden and she swore that she had seen the apparition clearly.

'What was the spectre like?' asked Lady Frances.

'It had the appearance of a m-man,' stammered poor Lady Jane. 'And its eyes were sunken and dark, and its face was pale as death, and its hair was wild like a madman's!'

'Was it in chains?' demanded Carmina eagerly. 'Had it got all its limbs? Did it drip with blood?'

'I did not wait to find out,' Lady Jane whimpered. 'I ran as soon as I saw it!'

'My lady!' It was Lord Culpepper and he sounded out of breath. Well, he is rather elderly – forty at least. 'What is amiss? Why did you run?'

Nobody bothered to answer him.

'You have made a poor show of protecting your companion, sir!' retorted Lady Frances as she helped Lady Jane to her feet.

Lord Culpepper stood there looking confused. He had obviously seen nothing except roses.

Mary Shelton and I took Lady Jane off to her bedchamber. I felt sorry for her – but I have to confess I badly wanted to hear more about the ghost. However, my hopes were dashed as soon as we came to Lady Jane's room, for Mrs Champernowne bustled up.

'What's all this to-do?' she enquired. 'What has happened? You look ill, my lady.' She felt Lady Jane's forehead.

Her concern soon turned to sternness, however, when we all tried at the same time to tell her about the ghost.

'I have already told you not to talk of such things!' she snapped. 'It is disrespectful to our host and certainly to Her Majesty. Now come with me, Lady Jane, and I'll make you a posset with a little mead and cinnamon in it.'

'But I did see a ghost,' mumbled Lady Jane.

'Nonsense!' snapped Mrs Champernowne. She put her arm around Lady Jane. ''Twas merely a figment of a summer fever that you have. I shall ask Her Majesty's physician to come and examine your humours. Mayhap your blood is running too hot and dry. Now,

we will have no more talk of ghosts, look you.'
She glared at us. 'If the Queen hears any of
this silly talk, her anger will be immeasurable.
Now get you gone and do not dare to say
another word on the matter.'

As she led Lady Jane away we heard fresh
wails from her. 'Where is my purse? I must
have dropped it in the Rose Garden. It had
my new lip paint in it!' she cried.

Mary Shelton and I went back down to the
main courtyard, where everyone was milling
around and whispering of the ghost. But I
didn't want to stand and talk about it; I wanted
to see it for myself!

Of course, I could not persuade any of my
fellow Maids to go back to the Rose Garden
with me to see if the spectre had reappeared.
They would not even cross the moat! But then
I saw a small figure with an armful of sheets
making her way through the crowds. It was
Ellie. Even at this time of night, she was
working. I slipped away from the others and
beckoned to her.

'You will never guess, Ellie,' I exclaimed

when she joined me, 'but Medenham Manor is haunted!'

'Don't say another word!' hissed Ellie urgently. 'I don't wish to hear any more. All the servants are talking about the ghost of the first Earl whenever they think they won't be overheard.'

'But I—' I was about to tell her about Lady Jane's scream, but Ellie interrupted.

'I've never seen a ghost and I never wish to,' she said fiercely, clutching her sheets in front of her as if they would stop a ghost in its tracks. 'And here we are, staying at a haunted house. I'll not have a wink of sleep. Ain't you scared, Grace?'

'No I'm not,' I declared. 'At least, not scared enough not to want to see it for myself. In truth, I am quite jealous of Lady Jane, for she saw it and I did not!'

Ellie looked amazed.

'But I am determined to change that,' I went on. 'Can you get a message to Masou? We must all three meet in the morning and plan how to get a sight of this ghost. Come to the

Kitchen Garden as soon as the clock strikes ten.'

'I'll try and be there,' whispered Ellie. 'But I warn you, Grace: no good can come of searching for spectres. 'Tis meddling with the Devil! And I'll be sure to get that stain out for you, my lady!' she finished, sinking into a deep curtsy.

I gawped at her and was just about to demand if she had gone quite mad when I heard footsteps. I turned to see Mrs Twiste the laundress coming across the courtyard towards us. Ellie must have seen her already and was cleverly playing the humble laundrymaid.

'Well met, Mrs Twiste,' I said, thinking quickly, 'for I would borrow Ellie Bunting in the morning. I have some ink stains to be removed that I do not wish Mrs Champernowne to see.'

Mrs Twiste's eyes twinkled. She is a kindly soul, unlike her deputy, Mrs Fadget, who is a miserable old cow and makes Ellie's life a misery.

'You do as Lady Grace asks, my girl,' she told Ellie. 'Ellie Bunting is a good worker, my lady, and will make a fine job of it,' she said to me.

I felt sly telling a lie to such a good person, and furthermore, suppose Mrs Twiste asks to see Ellie's work! Ah, but no matter — Ellie can show her a clean white chemise with no spots on it and Mrs Twiste will be even more pleased with her!

A minute later

I have just been rather naughty! I told the other Maids that I was ready to sleep and would now blow out the candle. Such squeals of protest I have never heard before! So I have agreed to leave the candle burning, but on one condition: that whenever I want to burn a candle at night in future, there will be no arguments.

'We will never complain again,' declared Lady Sarah. And all the others nodded and looked at me imploringly.

And now I, at least, intend to get a good night's sleep.

The Fifth Day of July, in the Year of Our Lord 1570

It is nearly noon and I am sitting cosily on a stool in the corner of the kitchen waiting for a 'treat', as Mrs Tiplady, the Cook's wife, calls it. Well, I have only had a few strawberries since breakfast and it has been quite a morning!

After breakfast the Queen summoned her Maids of Honour. She had got to hear of Lady Jane's spectral vision last night. We were very quiet and sheepish as we crept into the room the Queen has taken as her Presence Chamber. We could tell that Her Majesty was furious by the way she paced up and down the floor, and Lord Reynold was looking angry too, although not half so frightening. No one is as fearsome as the Queen when she is out of temper.

'Well, Lady Jane,' the Queen demanded, tapping her smartly with her fan. 'We would have you give some account of yourself. You have caused deep offence to your host and disturbance to my entire Court with your ridiculous behaviour last night in the Rose Garden!' She threw herself into her chair and squeezed her fan so hard that the feathers snapped and little rubies flew all over the floor.

Lady Jane paled under the Queen's glare. 'Your Majesty,' she gulped. 'Please forgive me. I was frightened. I thought I saw . . . that is . . . I caught sight of a—'

'You caught sight of nothing more than a shadow, foolish girl!' exclaimed the Queen, throwing the broken fan to the floor. 'And made a drama out of it! Is that not so?'

'I humbly beg Your Majesty's pardon,' mumbled Jane, 'and I ask forgiveness of Lord Reynold.'

Our host nodded solemnly.

'What I saw must have been a trick of the eye,' Lady Jane went on. 'Yes, now I remember, I was merely a little surprised at the illusion and dropped my purse. The story has flown round the Court since and . . . and has been much embroidered in the telling before it reached Your Majesty.'

My mouth dropped open with surprise. Lady Jane's story had changed completely! But I suppose it would be a brave person indeed who would dare contradict Her Majesty. At that moment I think Lady Jane would rather have been faced with the ghost than the Queen in her present temper.

Her Majesty suddenly turned on me. 'Why are you gaping like the carp in the moat, Lady Grace?' she snapped. 'Do you wish to add to the tale? Mayhap you saw a band of goblins in the gallery or a herd of cows flying over the roof?'

'No indeed, My Liege,' I assured her. 'I saw nothing that—'

'Then we shall have no more talk of these unnatural things,' said the Queen in a steely voice. 'Get you all gone from our sight!'

And with that we were dismissed.

As we hurried from the Presence Chamber, I realized that Ellie and Masou would be waiting for me in the Kitchen Garden as we had arranged. I raced up to my bedchamber to fetch a chemise, so that if anyone came near

I could pretend to be giving Ellie some sort of instruction about it. Then I stepped out of the north door at the rear of the house and set off to meet them.

As I walked through the Knot Garden, I paused for a moment to turn and gaze back at the old east wing. It had an abandoned look. There were some small mullioned windows, and there was a rough brick opening which must have had a door in it once. I was just picturing myself creeping in and exploring after dark when I heard a familiar voice.

'Grace!' It was Ellie coming from the laundry.

I shook myself out of my daydream. 'Come, walk with me, Ellie,' I said loudly in case anyone was within hearing. 'Here is the chemise I require your advice about.'

Ellie took the chemise and pretended to examine it as we went along a path over the moat and towards the Kitchen Garden.

Soon we came to a wooden door in a wall and Ellie pushed it open. We looked around furtively to make sure none of the gardeners were working nearby and then slipped through. Masou waved merrily at us from a strawberry bed.

We joined him and feasted on the lovely ripe strawberries. For a change, Ellie ate as daintily as a duchess, for she did not dare get stained with juice.

'That old misery guts, Mrs Fadget, will throw me into the starching vat if she thinks I've been eating strawberries,' Ellie said. 'She'll call me a thief for sure! And I cannot think of changing for these are the only clothes I have.'

Ellie's clothes are rough and full of holes. I long to give her one of my old kirtles but everyone would think she had stolen it and then she would be in terrible trouble.

When we had finished gorging ourselves we leaned against a wall in the warm sunshine. Masou loves the warm weather. Though he left Africa when he was very young, he is always happiest in the summer.

'So we have a ghost to find!' said Masou, grinning wickedly at Ellie. 'I wonder what terrible thing has woken it from its long sleep.'

'I believe that the gravedigger at St Augustine's Church may know the ghost's true story,' I said. 'I will tell you as soon I am able to go and—'

'I don't want to hear no more ghost stories!' interrupted Ellie with a wail.

Masou turned to me, his eyes sparkling with mischief. 'What a change of heart Mistress Ellie has had! She was pleading with me earlier to tell her about all the terrible spectres I saw during my childhood in Africa. Her favourite tale is about the drum that beat when no one was near, and drove the listeners to—'

'I never pleaded with you, Masou!' spluttered Ellie in outrage, covering her ears. 'Stop your stories! I told you I don't want to hear.'

'Or was it the terrible howling shroud that appears in the night?' teased Masou.

'Stow it, Masou!' snapped Ellie.

'No, I remember now,' Masou went on. 'It was the one about the headless camel from Khartoum!'

'Enough of these African ghosts!' I laughed. 'You should not tease Ellie like this.'

'Thank you, Grace,' said Ellie, relieved.

''Tis a pleasure, Ellie,' I replied. 'Now let us consider how we are to find the ghost of Medenham Manor that walks the east wing and frightens Maids of Honour.'

'By all the saints!' exclaimed Ellie. 'Don't you start, Grace!'

'You do not need to come on our ghost hunt,' I assured her. 'But for my part, I am determined to go and lie in wait for the spectre – if I can get away this evening.'

'I shall not let you go alone, Grace,' declared Masou, sticking out his chest and looking bold. 'You will need me to protect you in case it is an evil spirit. And fear not, for though it will be a dangerous undertaking, I am brave enough for the task!'

'*Brave*, Masou?' I grinned. 'You are just nosy, like me.'

'Well, I'm not going to be brave nor nosy,' snorted Ellie. 'But I'll come with you to stop you both doing anything daft.'

'Then you are truly brave, Ellie,' said Masou. 'Come, I shall restore your good humour. Let me show you a feat that no one else in the world can do, and that no living soul has ever seen before! Pray silence for Masou the Amazing!'

Ellie grinned. 'Go on then,' she said. 'Amaze us!'

'You must sit here on the path,' Masou told her. 'Now, whatever you do, stay as still as a statue.'

Puzzled, Ellie sat down on the grass where Masou had indicated while he walked to the other end of the path. There he stopped, turned and began to run straight towards her! Ellie shrieked and covered her head with her arms, but just as I thought Masou was sure to run her down, he leaped right over her, curling into a neat ball and turning not one, but two somersaults! He flew over Ellie and three blackcurrant bushes before he landed. Then he bounded back to join us with a broad grin on his face.

'Don't you ever do that again, you varmint!'

shouted Ellie, struggling to her feet and shaking her fists at him.

'But it was wonderful, Ellie,' I gasped. 'An incredible sight to see!'

'Not from underneath it weren't,' grumbled Ellie. 'I thought I was going to be squashed!'

'You must retire at once,' I told Masou, 'for you could not do anything better, unless you jump over the moat!'

Masou stood and thought for a moment. 'That is what I will do,' he said solemnly, kneeling at my feet with his hands clasped over his heart. 'Anything for my favourite lady!'

'Don't be silly, Masou!' I protested. 'I only spoke in jest. No one could somersault that far.'

'And if you don't make it,' added Ellie, 'them carp will have you for dinner!'

'Then I am even more determined to do it!' declared Masou, springing to his feet. 'But now I think I should beat a hasty retreat, before someone discovers what I did to the cucumber beds when I landed!'

Giggling, we all hurried away.

'Meet me in the Rose Garden straight after nightfall,' I said to my friends as we parted at the door of the Kitchen Garden.

'We must be mad!' muttered Ellie, then disappeared towards the laundry, clutching my chemise.

Masou laughed and cartwheeled away to practise with the rest of the tumbling troupe. And I made my way to the kitchen.

In truth I only meant to come here for just a moment as I wished to make myself known to Mrs Bridget Tiplady. Until she married she spent all her life at Wellworth Hall – the very place where my mother was born.

I had wondered if I might then go down to the churchyard to see Ben Boggis and hear the true story of the first Earl's death before Mrs Champernowne noticed I was gone, but Mrs Tiplady was so pleased to see me that I did not have the heart to hurry away.

When I introduced myself, she curtsied and beamed delightedly at me. 'I am honoured, my lady,' she said, wiping her hands on her apron. 'And may I say how much you favour your poor dear mother? I remember her as a girl and she was just as you are now, with her bright smile and friendly ways. She would often come and talk to me when I was working.' She gave a chuckle. 'I recall she was always hungry!'

I smiled as I pictured my mother so young and full of life – and with an appetite just like mine! But I couldn't help feeling sad too, as I always do when I think of how I miss her.

'I am sorry, my lady,' said Mrs Tiplady, when she saw my face cloud over. 'I should not have talked of her. I was that grieved when I found out about her passing.'

'Please do not make apology,' I said. 'I am very glad to speak of her with you.'

'And I warrant you'd be glad to taste a little something,' she said, smiling, 'if you have the same appetite as your mother. I am about to decorate some white leche especially for Her Majesty. I think I could spare a little for you. Sit you there away from the bustle and I will fetch it when it is ready.' She turned away, then came back to me and whispered, 'And I shall make a cream and almond tart for supper soon. It was your mother's favourite!' And off she went again.

So I came to sit in this corner and have decided to write in my daybooke while I wait for my treat. I love white leche. It is so sweet and sticky. Indeed, it is almost impossible to concentrate on writing for the wonderful smell of it! And now I see Mrs Tiplady approaching with some for me. Wonderful! I shall thank her and be gone.

Late – in a small storeroom

I cannot quite believe all that has happened this evening! I have come to a little storeroom off the gallery above the Great Hall so that I can think straight and write it all down sensibly.

I am sure that Lord Reynold would not mind me sitting among his paintings. I am perched next to a woman holding a monkey – though the expression on the woman's face makes it hard to see which is meant to be the monkey and which the lady! I have heard that Lord Reynold will be unveiling a portrait of Her Majesty as a young girl. He has recently bought it and is going to give it pride of place – in honour of her visit, of course. Perhaps he took the monkey portrait down to make room. I do hope the royal one is not by the same artist!

Well, after supper I had to find an excuse to leave the Great Hall. Since my leg hadn't fallen off and I didn't have the plague, I had to use the old excuse of a headache. I must have managed to make myself look quite ill, for to my surprise Mrs Champernowne did not doubt me. In fact I play-acted too well and it was all I could do to stop her helping me up to my bedchamber and slapping poultices on my forehead!

I left the Great Hall and made as if to go to the stairs. Then, when I was certain no one was looking, I turned round and crept out of a door into the main courtyard. It was darker tonight. No torches had been lit as none of the Court wished to venture out after yesterday. However, the sky was clear and the moon was almost full. It gave some light but cast odd shadows about me.

Above my head I heard the clock strike ten. I hoped Masou and Ellie were waiting. Although I desperately wanted to see the ghost, I found I did not want to see it on my own! As I reached the bridge to cross the moat into the Rose Garden, I heard a strange echoing moan. But I wasn't fooled.

'Come out, you two,' I sighed. 'You cannot scare me that easily!'

Ellie and Masou popped up from the far end of the bridge.

'See, Masou,' said Ellie. 'I told you it wouldn't work, you beetle-brain!'

'It was worth a try nonetheless!' Masou grinned.

We crept together through the Rose Garden round to the far side of the east wing. It seemed rather eerie without the bustle of the courtiers, and the silver moonlight didn't help.

I gazed at the old east wing. It was dark

against the sky and looked empty and desolate. The windows were like sightless eyes, since much of the glass had been removed, and parts of the roof were missing too.

And there, at last, I saw the oriel window! It jutted out from the building and I could just make out the ledge above. The little wall round it was shaped like the battlements of a castle, just as the old gravedigger had described it, and behind was a dark hole in the wall where a window had once been. I was sure this must be the very place where the ghost had appeared to Lady Jane. I felt a shiver of excitement.

'Come!' I whispered. 'Let us hide behind these bushes.'

The three of us crouched together in the darkness. Through the leaves we could see the top of the oriel window clearly in the moonlight. We waited and we watched and we waited and we watched some more. We heard the clock strike the quarter, the half, the three quarters and then eleven.

'Are you sure this is the place?' asked Masou

at last. 'If it does not appear soon I shall fall asleep in spite of these thorns!'

'Lady Jane described the ledge above the oriel window perfectly,' I insisted. 'And it is spoken of in all the old stories.'

'Let's go,' said Ellie, starting to get to her feet. 'We've waited long enough. The more I think about this ghost, the more scared I get!'

'Don't be frightened, Ellie,' I said, squeezing her hand to comfort her. 'Perhaps Lady Jane saw only shadows. Perhaps there is no ghost, and the first Earl ran away to Cornwall as Lord Reynold would have us believe.'

But Ellie didn't answer: she was frozen to the spot, her eyes wide with fright and her hand pointing to the east wing.

I followed her gaze. There on the ledge above the oriel window stood a figure dressed in tattered clothes with a ragged white ruff. But this was no earthly man. The figure glowed in the moonlight, and made no sound but stared sightlessly out over the moat.

I found myself staring open-mouthed, for I was looking at a real ghost! Ellie buried her face in my shoulder and shivered with fear.

'By Allah!' hissed Masou. 'What manner of foul thing is that?'

'We must get a closer look,' I whispered, trying not to let my voice shake. But as I spoke the ghost moved back to the wall and vanished in the shadows.

For a moment we were silent. Then Masou stood up. 'I never thought to see a spectre for myself!' he muttered uneasily.

Ellie jumped to her feet and shook her finger at him. 'You never seen a ghost?' she demanded in anger. 'You told me all those tales of the terrible things you saw in Africa and filled my head with fear, and all along you were telling me fibble-fabble!'

'I am deeply sorry,' said Masou, serious for once. 'They were indeed stories and not true in the least.'

We looked at the place where the ghost had stood.

'Do you think it truly was the ghost of the first Earl?' asked Masou.

'There are many strange stories about

Medenham Manor,' I said, 'and they all tell of the same spectre. That of the first Earl, who disappeared a hundred years ago and no one knows why.'

'Most likely he was murdered,' quavered Ellie.

'And for ever seeks vengeance on his murderer,' added Masou mysteriously. 'That is why his ghost walks.'

'Or he killed himself,' suggested Ellie, looking at the window as if she expected the phantom to reappear at any moment, 'and may not rest in peace as punishment for taking his own life.'

'One thing is for certain,' I said. 'The first Earl never ran off to Cornwall, else why would he haunt the east wing of his old manor? I think he must have met with a violent end here in this house. For some reason he has begun to walk again now that the building work has started, and I am going to find out why, if only for Lord Reynold's sake. But I must do it before Her Majesty storms off and takes the whole Court with her!'

'In the country where I was born,' said Masou thoughtfully, 'it is said that there is only one way to be rid of a ghost.'

'Not another of your tales, Masou!' groaned Ellie, as we began to walk back to the manor.

'No indeed,' insisted Masou. 'Upon my life, this is true. In order to lay a ghost to rest you must first find out what is disturbing its peace.'

'How do you do that?' demanded Ellie, glancing nervously over her shoulder.

'You simply go and ask it what is wrong!' said Masou.

'Not me!' declared Ellie firmly. 'I ain't talkin' to no ghost! People shouldn't meddle with the dead. Mayhap the old Earl just wants to be left alone – him and his house too. Lord Reynold should never have started to pull the manor down. It's not right when his ancestor is dead and don't have no say in the matter!'

'That may be true, Ellie,' I said. 'But if it is, then we are too late, for much of the work has already been done. But if the ghost walks for some other reason then perchance we can help. We must discover what troubles him. Ben

Boggis, the gravedigger, may know, but I cannot be sure of getting away to see him.'

'One of the servants may know the true story,' said Masou. 'Ellie and I will try to find out.'

'Have a care,' I said, as we crossed the bridge and made to part. 'All talk of the ghost is forbidden, so you will have to enquire secretly.'

'You are speaking to the master of discretion!' Masou declared proudly.

I feel sorry for the old Earl, if he is indeed the ghost. It cannot be much fun floating around a house that is being demolished – especially if no one will admit you are even there! I am sure it is my duty as Lady Pursuivant to solve this mystery. And I am sure that even the ghost will be grateful if he can be laid to rest. Although I cannot fathom how I will achieve this. I have no experience in dealing with the dead. No matter. It must be done.

Tomorrow I shall start by speaking to Lady Jane. I want more details about what the ghost did when it appeared and whether it spoke.

She may have remembered more now that she's not so frightened.

The woman with the monkey is staring at me from her painting. I have had enough of her. I shall go to bed.

The Sixth Day of July, in the Year of Our Lord 1570

In the armoury

I am perched on a small window seat behind the 'elephant' armour that startled me two days ago. It is the most perfect place to sit and write, for no one can see me here. It is about eleven in the morning. I have been investigating until I nearly burst – and there is still more to do if I am to get to the truth of the Medenham ghost!

Earlier this morning I stalked Lady Jane like a cat stalking a mouse. I was waiting for a moment when she was not with some young gentleman or other. Hell's teeth! I should have known it would be nigh on impossible. Wherever she went, her faithful admirers followed, tripping over each other to be noticed. She may complain that Lady Sarah has all the suitors but she seems to have plenty buzzing around. Finally, as one sighing courtier left her side and before another could approach, I leaped out in front of her from an alcove in the passage. She shrieked with horror as I appeared and told me I had frightened her witless.

'I am sorry,' I apologized, just about keeping my face straight. 'I was most thoughtless, for you have had one fright already and must be feeling fearful!' I was pleased with myself. This was a clever way to lead straight into the business of the ghost.

My lady looked agitated. 'I do not know what you mean, Grace,' she said, glancing round to make sure no one could hear what we were talking about. 'If you are referring to that silly moment two nights since, I do not wish to speak of it.'

'But everyone heard you scream,' I insisted. 'You must have seen something strange or you would not have cried out like that.'

This was not strictly true. Lady Jane can be a fine shrieker when she wants the sympathy of the young men, but the cry in the Rose Garden had not been play-acting.

Lady Jane tried in vain to sound light-hearted. 'What a fuss to make over a Maid of Honour losing her bag!' She laughed weakly. 'I am surprised at you taking an interest in such a trifling thing, Grace.'

'But why did you say you had seen a ghost?' I persisted. 'There surely must have been something there on the ledge.' I checked the passageway was empty. 'There is no one to overhear,' I whispered conspiratorially. 'You can tell me.'

But Lady Jane was not to be swayed. 'It was a shadow in the moonlight, I assure you,' she answered firmly. Then she looked down the passage and stamped her foot. 'There now, Grace, you have pestered me so long that Mr Winterbottom has given me up and gone elsewhere!'

'Then why do you not follow him?' I suggested, with an innocent look.

'I certainly shall not!' snapped my lady. 'I have no wish for his company!' And she swept off in the opposite direction.

Lady Jane's explanation about the ghost

made no sense. I knew it could not have been a shadow in the moonlight, for there had been no moonlight at the time! The clouds had been covering the moon. Lady Jane had changed her story, either because she feared the Queen's wrath, or because the thought of the apparition was too terrible to her.

I was not going to give up though, for I am determined to find out the true story of this ghost. But who could I ask next? Then I thought of Lord Reynold. The very person! I knew I could not mention the ghost itself, for he is insistent that no such thing exists. However, I could ask about his family history and find out more about the first Earl. With luck I might be able to uncover some dark secret!

I found Lord Reynold in the gallery. He was directing two red-faced servants, who were staggering from one side of a fireplace to the other, holding a large portrait covered in a cloth.

'Ah, Lady Grace.' He beamed. 'Mayhap you can advise me. Where does the light fall best for this portrait of the Queen? I would not want Her Gracious Majesty to be in shadow.'

And nor would the Queen herself, I thought! I knew I must help him, for I would get nowhere with my business until his was sorted out. I made sure I looked thoughtful.

'In honour of Her Majesty,' I said, knowing this would most likely settle the matter, 'I would put the portrait here, where it will have the best view of your glorious Knot Garden, my lord, and where it will be seen in good light without the sun fading it.' I pointed to a spot on the wall to the right of the fireplace.

'The very thing!' declared the Earl, to the obvious relief of the two servants, who put their burden down and began measuring the wall.

Lord Reynold pulled up the cloth and showed me the picture. 'Do you think the Queen will look favourably upon the portrait?'

'Oh yes,' I said truthfully. It was a beautiful painting, showing Her Majesty when she was about my age. She wore a red gown with sleeves and forepart of raised gold brocade, and the simple neckline was edged with a thin strip of gold. The sleeves were pointed and quite old-fashioned. She was holding a prayer book in her hand and there was not a monkey in sight!

I wondered how I could bring the subject round to the first Earl. I moved casually to a portrait of a man dressed very much in the style of the old King Henry. 'Is this your father, my lord?' I asked. 'I see a resemblance.'

Lord Reynold nodded. 'Yes, that is the fourth Earl of Medenham, painted by Hans Holbein, no less.'

I moved on to the next painting. 'Could this be your grandfather?'

'Indeed, Lady Grace.' Lord Reynold smiled. 'You have a keen eye. And here,' he said, moving along to another gentleman in old-fashioned finery, 'is my great-grandfather.'

'Now, have I got this right?' I said, pretending to look puzzled. 'You, my lord, are the fifth Earl of Medenham. And here we have the fourth, third and second earls. That leaves only the first. Have you a portrait of him too?'

Lord Reynold's face clouded as he took me to the far corner of the gallery. There in the shadows hung a small painting. 'This is the only surviving portrait of the first Earl,' he said shortly.

I peered hard into the gloom. It was a terrible painting and it was cracked and peeling. I could just make out a faded figure in a round-necked tunic and cloak, with a loose hat that hung in a point on his shoulder.

'Do tell me about him,' I said sweetly.

'He built the manor, you know,' Lord Reynold told me. 'He had a fine eye for architecture by all accounts, and of course he began the family arms business.' Then he backed away from the portrait as if disgusted with it. ''Tis a shame he besmirched the memory of the Waldegraves,' he muttered. 'He should never have run off with his strumpet and left these beautiful estates to the mercy of gossipmongers. It gave rise to all sorts of silly stories about what happened to him.'

I said nothing as I did not want to disturb his train of thought. This was interesting.

'His son was only a young man at the time,' he went on, 'and it was a huge task for him to take over as head of the family with all its heavy duties as armourer to the King.'

I decided to take a leaf out of Lady Jane's book, and play the simpering maid. 'I confess I have heard the stories about the first Earl's mistress,' I said, giggling a little, 'but I did not know if they were true.'

'Indeed they are,' said Lord Reynold firmly. 'And there, I hope, is an end to the matter.'

We moved to the windows that looked out over the Knot Garden and the river beyond. I felt sorry for my host. All he wanted to do was create a new house and entertain his monarch. Yet to do so, he had to stick to his story about his ancestor running away with his mistress. He must have known that if his builders believed there was a ghost nearby they might consider the manor cursed and refuse to return and finish their work. I could see that I would get no further with my questioning, and I did not want any word of my inquisitiveness to reach the Queen, so I decided to change the subject in the hope that Lord Reynold would forget I had asked about the old Earl at all.

'I hear there is to be a feast tonight in honour of Her Majesty,' I said.

Lord Reynold perked up at this and rubbed his hands with glee. 'A very fine one,' he told me. 'There will be stuffed peacock with the beak painted gold and the tail feathers in full display, and roasted carp from my very own moat. And Mrs Tiplady will make her famous cream and almond tart.'

He went on to list more sumptuous dishes that his kitchens would serve and added that he wished there had been time to erect a proper banqueting hall, as befitted Her Gracious Majesty. But it seemed Her Gracious Majesty had told him to cease worrying, for the Great Hall would do very well for all the courses. I admit I did not pay close attention: I was thinking of other things.

'The feast sounds magnificent,' I told Lord Reynold, 'but for now I must not intrude upon your precious time any further.' I curtsied and left him thinking happily about his feast. I was glad to see his good humour restored. Lord Reynold is so much more pleasant when he is jolly. He reminds me of a dear old dog, always happy to see you and anxious to please. (If he had a tail I am sure it would wag his whole body!)

So it seemed no one at Medenham Manor would give me any clue as to why the first Earl's ghost should walk. There was only one thing for it: I decided I must see the gravedigger, Ben Boggis.

Now that my daybooke is up to date, I shall go forthwith. But I cannot go alone, so I will find Mary Shelton and persuade her to go with me. I will tell her I feel a sudden need to pray.

Ye Gods! I had forgotten that it is nearly time for dinner. My head has been so full of hauntings that I have ignored the rumblings of my poor stomach! My visit to Ben Boggis will have to wait until this afternoon.

After three of the clock

I am sitting in the dressing room that lies between Lady Jane and Carmina's bedchamber and mine. It is full of trunks, mostly Lady Sarah's, but I have made myself a comfortable perch on a thick cloak on the floor and I think I shall not be disturbed. The other Maids are with the rest of the Court on the grass close to the Rose Garden, being entertained by our host. I will join them as soon as I have finished writing.

After dinner I made straight for Mary Shelton and asked her to accompany me to the church for some praying.

'Of course, Grace,' said Mary Shelton with a smile, 'though I confess I am a little surprised. It is not like you to seek the quiet of a church.'

I just smiled and she asked no more. That is what I like about Mary Shelton. She never questions when I ask her to do something for me.

We asked Mrs Champernowne's leave to go and she looked at me most suspiciously. She always thinks I am up to something! (She is usually right of course.)

'Very well,' she grunted at last, pursing her lips. 'But look you are back within the hour. The Court will be gathering outside to listen to some of our host's poetry.'

I groaned inwardly. Lord Reynold is a dear man but I doubt he will make a fine poet!

Mary Shelton and I walked down to the church and knelt in Lord Reynold's pew for a goodly time. Mary prayed devoutly, but I confess I was thinking more about how I could get away to speak to the gravedigger.

In fact it was Mary who came to my rescue! After she had prayed her fill and we were leaving the church, she saw the old man digging a grave on the far side of the church-yard. 'Look, Grace,' she said. 'There is Ben Boggis, who told us those eerie stories. Do you remember?'

'Of course I do. And you have had to sleep with a lit candle ever since!' I reminded her. I was pretending to joke, but inside I was very excited. Here was my chance to find out more about the first Earl.

'That was not because of *his* words,' Mary assured me. 'It is Lady Jane who has worked us up into this fine state. But for all that, I love to hear a strange tale.'

'Well now you can,' I said eagerly, leading her along the path towards the old man. 'Unless you are too frightened, that is,' I added mischievously.

'I will not be scared,' Mary assured me, 'for the sky is blue and the birds are singing. I am happy to hear a ghost story.'

At that moment the gravedigger saw us. Immediately he stopped digging and climbed out of the hole.

'Welcome, young ladies,' he called in his croaky voice. 'I wager you've come back to hear old Ben tell you the true story of the first Earl of Medenham.'

Mary and I nodded eagerly as we made our way over to him.

'Then you are talking to the right man,' he said, leaning on his spade, 'for us Boggises have always known what happened up at Medenham Manor.'

'And how is that?' I asked eagerly.

Old Ben chuckled and looked sly. 'Not only did we have the burying of all around,' he told us, 'but my great-great-grandma were a maid at the manor in the first Earl's time, and she were in the confidence of his manservant. She always told how the first Earl was a fair master. But 'twas a troubled time. There had been fighting over the throne between those who followed the House of Lancaster and those who followed the House of York, and the first Earl was wealthy because of it. That made other men jealous. So you could say he had enemies.' He paused for dramatic effect. I could see he was enjoying his tale. He would do well in Mr Somers's troupe. 'But none more so,' he went on with relish, 'than his own son! 'Twas always said the lad was a shady character. Though you'd never know it if you talked to Lord Reynold.'

'Indeed not,' I put in. 'He paints a picture of the second Earl as a decent, hardworking man.'

'But my family have kept the truth alive,' continued Ben Boggis. 'The story is passed down from father to son.' He stopped to scratch his beard.

'Please go on,' urged Mary, wide-eyed with interest.

'Well, one day the first Earl disappeared and were never seen again. His son put out the story that he had run away to Cornwall with his mistress and that's what folk had to believe. There was talk of course. But King Edward, the fourth of that name, looked kindly upon the Earl's son and none dared speak of the rumours.'

'So what really happened to the first Earl?' I asked, hoping I did not sound too impatient.

Ben Boggis gave a gravelly chuckle. 'What I am about to tell you is the truth, so help me. The truth that only us Boggises know, for my great-great-grandma had it from the first Earl's man afore he fled in fear of his life.'

Mary Shelton gasped at that and Ben nodded approvingly, pleased with the effect his tale was having.

'It is time the truth were told,' he continued solemnly, 'now the ghost walks again. The first Earl were an open-handed man, fair to his servants and generous to his family. But this weren't good enough for his eldest son. That young man had greed in his very soul and couldn't wait to get his hands on his inheritance. He found out that his father had a secret chamber where he kept all his money — and there was a good deal of it, believe you me. One fateful day he followed the Earl there, all quiet like, so as he shouldn't be heard. And as soon as his father stepped inside the room, he slammed the door shut on him and wedged it so that he had no chance of escape. The walls were thick, the Earl's cries went unheard and his own son left him there to starve to death!'

He watched our shocked faces for a moment. 'Only the first Earl's man knew what had happened and he was too afraid to stay and speak out. But he told my great-great-grandma what he knew before he left and she told her own family. The second Earl, he must have gone back into that room once more to take all the money, for he was never short o' riches. But soon after the first Earl disappeared, his ghost was seen at the manor. And I believe the Medenham family is cursed and will be until the truth is revealed.'

'But the ghost has not walked for a hundred years,' I said. 'Why is he walking again now? And why does he appear on that ledge?'

'As to why he walks, that I cannot say,' Ben Boggis answered, shaking his head. 'Only the ghost himself can tell you. But it was said that the first Earl was often seen on that ledge when he was alive. He liked the view of his Rose Garden and the village beyond.'

Mary touched my arm. I could feel her hand shaking. 'It is time we were returning to the manor,' she said quietly. 'Her Majesty will soon be finished with her business and looking for our attendance.'

We thanked the gravedigger for his time and gave him a few coins.

'At your service, my ladies,' he said, touching his cap. Then he looked up at the cloudless sky. 'Take care now. There'll be a storm by nightfall, mark my words.' And he shuffled off back to his digging.

'He tells a thrilling ghost story,' said Mary, as we walked back to the house. 'I am determined not to dwell on it overmuch, however, particularly tonight.' She gave a shudder. 'Walled up alive!' she exclaimed. 'No wonder the old Earl's ghost returned to haunt the place where he met such a terrible end!'

'It would be a reason to haunt,' I agreed, 'but I do not think Ben Boggis is right about the family being cursed. The Waldegraves have done nothing but prosper since the time of the first Earl!' I spoke lightly, for Mary Shelton did not need to know that I was investigating the mystery. In truth I was excited by what we had heard and I could not wait to try and find the secret chamber Ben Boggis had mentioned.

'You are right,' Mary said. Then she fanned her face and changed the subject. 'It is becoming hotter and hotter.'

'And sticky too!' I agreed. 'Heat like this often comes before a storm. Mayhap Ben Boggis knew the truth about the weather at least!'

As we approached Medenham Manor, we could see the Court beginning to gather on the grass by the Rose Garden for the poetry reading. Canopies and cushions had been placed there and in the middle was a grand chair for the Queen.

'Oh dear.' I giggled. 'I expect all the poems will be in honour of Her Majesty.' I have noticed that many courtiers believe themselves to be poets, especially when they have the Queen as their inspiration!

'Now, do not make jest of Lord Reynold,' Mary Shelton said sternly, but I could see the laughter in her eyes. 'Come, let us join the others.' She linked her arm in mine as we crossed the grass.

But in truth I had too much to do to be listening to poetry. I decided I had to make an excuse. 'I have just remembered that I must seek out Mrs Twiste!' I exclaimed hurriedly. 'I have an ink stain on one of the wrist ruffs

I wore yesterday and I would have her deal with it. I must go now else Mrs Champer-nowne will find out. You know how cross she gets when I have an accident with my day-booke and penner. I will come back as soon as I can and hear Lord Reynold's adoring poetry.'

'Would that I had such a stain,' said Mary, casting a rueful look towards our host. 'I fear I will feel drowsy – with the heat, of course. Good luck with your endeavours, Grace.' She went off slowly to sit with the other Maids.

I had told Mary the truth – well, nearly. I *did* wish to see a laundress, but not for my wrist ruffs. I quickly found a young page and instructed him to send Ellie Bunting to my chamber without delay. He scuttled off and I made my way to my room. How much easier it would be if Ellie could be my tiring woman. Then I could speak to her whenever I want and I wouldn't have to pretend to have made quite so many ink stains.

I sat and fidgeted for what seemed like ages, but at long last there was a knock at the door and Ellie's face peeped round it.

'You asked for me, my lady,' she said, playing the proper servant and bobbing a curtsy. 'I came as fast as I could.'

'It's all right,' I told her quickly. 'There's no one else here.'

Ellie scampered in, grinning. I had a wrist ruff ready to thrust under her nose if anyone else came along. We sat on the bed together and shared the white leche that Mrs Tiplady had given me yesterday. It was delicious – sweet and smooth and sticky, with sugared rose petals on top.

'Ooh,' sighed Ellie, running her tongue around her mouth, 'that was lovely!'

I feel guilty sometimes because I never go hungry – well, only when I am too busy to eat – but Ellie is always in need of food. I looked at her skinny arms. Then I noticed that she had a large bruise just above one elbow.

'Where did you get that?' I asked, passing her the last piece of leche.

She took it gratefully. 'Old Fadget caught me this morning,' she said with her mouth full. 'She told me she couldn't find me last night and wanted to know where I'd been. She pinched me arm really hard and shook me till my teeth rattled. For a moment I thought of telling 'er about the ghost and scaring the petticoats off 'er, but talk of the haunting is forbidden.' She rubbed her arm. 'She's always nipping at me for nothing.'

Poor Ellie has such a miserable time with Mrs Fadget. I gave her a quick hug. 'Have you found out anything about the ghost?' I asked.

'All the servants are whispering in corners and I've strained me ears till me head's nearly come off me shoulders,' said Ellie. 'But they're not saying anything worth hearing, they're just frightening each other. How about you, Grace?'

I told her the story that Ben Boggis had related with such gusto and Ellie was wide-eyed when I'd finished.

'I am keen to search for the secret chamber, but as for the ghost I think Masou has the right of it,' I said, 'and there is only one way to find out what it wants. We must face it and ask why it walks the east wing!'

'No, Grace!' Ellie gasped, jumping to her feet. 'That would be mad. I think the summer heat has turned your head. Talking to ghosts! It ain't right. You'll be cursed and bewitched and . . . and . . .' She paused for breath, and I was about to tell her not to worry when she started up again! '. . . and you'll bring all sorts of evil goblins and demons down upon you!' she finished.

I caught her hands. 'Don't worry, Ellie,' I said. 'I am not scared of the ghost. Indeed, I am determined to seek it out and speak to it tonight. But you do not have to come, especially as you may risk the wrath of Mrs Fadget. Masou will accompany me.'

'You're daft, the pair of you!' exclaimed Ellie. 'You're mazed in the head. Don't come running to me for help when you've been scared to death!'

I could not help laughing at that and after a moment Ellie realized what she had said and joined in.

'I have one request of you,' I told her. 'Please take a message to Masou and ask him to join me at the back of the east wing tonight just before ten. You know, by the Knot Garden. I have seen a way in there.'

Ellie agreed and went back to the laundry. And now I must leave my daybooke and my comfortable perch and go and listen to Lord Reynold's poetry, for it would be rude to miss it all. Although I think I would prefer to join Ellie at her starching vat!

In my bedchamber, late in the evening

It is well after ten of the clock and I am rushing to get down to the feast before it is entirely over. I have missed most of it already, but it was worth it. I have just got into my gown and Fran has been in and tied my sleeves on – nice and tightly this time! As soon as I have finished writing I will go to the Great Hall.

It has been an extraordinary evening. When I rejoined the other Maids this afternoon, it seemed that Lord Reynold had only just got into his stride and so I had not missed much of his poetry after all – unfortunately. I sat down on a cushion next to a slumbering Mary Shelton and nudged her awake in case she began to snore. Mary is like a horse and can doze sitting up!

Lord Reynold had much enthusiasm but lacked some skill at rhyme. As he began an ode to 'Our Fair Elizabeth, Ruler of Our Hearts', I thought about my plan to seek out the ghost again.

He had walked two nights in a row, and I was hoping he would do the same tonight. But I knew this evening was to be the feast Lord Reynold had spoken of, and it was likely to go on until very late. If I crept out after the feast – as I did after supper last night – I feared I would be too late to see the ghost. There was only one thing to do: I decided I would have to leave the feast early, or not attend it at all! But I would need an excuse to behave so, and I could not feign another headache – one of these days my lies will catch up with me and I will be punished with such a megrim that I will not be able to lift my head from my pillow! I wondered about pretending to be locked in my bedchamber, but then I remembered that there is no lock on our door. Perhaps I could say I was too scared to leave the room on account of the haunting. But no, that would not do, for there must be no mention of the ghost.

Lord Reynold was now reciting 'Elizabeth the Huntress'. 'With her gallant steed and her dogs with their loyal noses,' he intoned, 'she shall chase after stags and fleet of foot does-es!'

Dear Lord Reynold! He had given me an idea. Her Majesty dotes on her dogs and so of course they have to come on progress with her. I guessed they had been shut up with little exercise since our arrival, so I thought I would offer to take them for a walk. It was a good excuse, but it meant I would need to be outside early: I could not get the dogs and set off on a ghost hunt straight away. That would be cruel to the poor little things, who expect a good run whenever they see me. No, I would have to make the supreme sacrifice and miss the *whole* feast! It was a shame, but I could see no other course of action.

I decided I would not offer my services to the Queen until just before the feast, otherwise she might send me out straight away and scupper my plans. I had to bide my time. Then I realized Her Majesty had risen, and I jumped to my feet with the rest of the Court.

'For myself I would listen to your words all day, Lord Reynold!' she said. 'But these young girls have not put a needle to their embroidery for at least a week. I cannot have my Maids of Honour becoming lazy.'

I think I can speak for all when I say that we were very glad to escape the poetry and sit in the cool Presence Chamber doing our stitching. I am working on a cover for a cushion – a nice summer scene – and I have been enjoying it, but it has rather too many tiny flowers to concentrate on when your mind is occupied with catching ghosts. I hope I manage to finish this piece. The robin I was doing a while ago somehow got ink stains on him – I can't imagine how! – and had to be abandoned in the end.

When it was almost time to change for supper I approached the Queen and sank to the floor in a curtsy.

'Yes, Grace?' She smiled. 'What do you want, my dear?'

'Your Majesty,' I said, 'I have come to beg your permission to take your dogs out for some exercise.'

'But do you not know the time?' the Queen asked in surprise. 'You will be late for the grand feast that Lord Reynold has promised.'

The Queen knows my healthy appetite and I must admit I was suffering some anxiety about missing a meal.

'I will make sure I do not miss *all* of supper, Your Majesty,' I said. 'I would have asked you sooner but it has only just occurred to me that the dogs must be in sore need of a walk and I feel guilty that I have not thought of them before.'

The Queen looked hard at me. I thought she had guessed that I had some other purpose in mind. But before she could question me I hurried on. 'I have to admit that I am not only thinking of Philip, Ivan and Henri,' I confessed. 'In truth I am so hot I doubt I could eat a morsel! I would be grateful for some fresh evening air.'

'Now we have the truth, Grace' – the Queen smiled – 'and I wish I had the freedom to accompany you. Get you gone then! But look you return for the banqueting course. I believe that cream and almond tart is to be served and it was your dear mother's favourite.'

I wish the Queen hadn't reminded me! But I made haste for my bedchamber and changed into my oldest kirtle.

Philip, Henri and Ivan were so pleased to see me that they barked excitedly and turned circles in delight. I took them up the hill in front of the house. It was still very humid, and the light was fading as they scampered through the trees and chased sticks. I had to give them a long walk for I needed them to be tired and docile when I met Masou. Old Ben Boggis had been right about a storm coming. There was a full moon tonight, but I could see dark clouds gathering on the horizon.

I listened out for the courtyard clock, which chimes every fifteen minutes. When I heard the quarter before ten, I put the dogs back on their leashes and made my way down the hill towards the manor.

I reached the back of the house to find that there were torches placed in sconces on the outside wall of the Great Hall. And I could hear laughter and chatter coming from the feast within. My stomach rumbled as I thought of all the delicious food, but I ignored it and crossed over a small bridge to make my way through the Knot Garden and over to the broken doorway in the east wing.

Suddenly there was a rustling in the hedge by my side that nearly made me jump. Then I realized that none of the dogs seemed bothered. In fact, Henri was wagging his tail.

'Come out, Masou!' I called. 'I know it's you.'

And indeed, out popped Masou. The dogs bounced around him in delight. And then, without warning, another head popped out of the bush, making me jump properly this time!

'Don't be scared, Grace,' said a familiar voice. ''Tis only me.'

'I am not frightened!' I said hotly, as Ellie came into view. 'I was not expecting to see you, that is all.'

'Well, I wasn't going to be left out,' she declared. I saw that she was holding a large bag in her hand which she twisted nervously. 'Besides, I couldn't let you face the ghost on your own,' she went on. 'I knew you wouldn't take the proper precautions. You need me for that.' She delved into the bag. 'Lucky amulets!' she announced, pulling out various herbs and plants. 'Now, Masou, you take the garlic and marjoram; Grace, you can have the vervain and the bay, and I'll hold the basil. That little lot should ward off the evil eye. And I've got an elf-shot,' she added, triumphantly pulling a little carved, pointed flint out of the bag. 'Fairies made this, you know. I found it in a field and Mrs Hollowbread, the laundress here at Medenham, told me it was a lucky find and would protect me from evil.'

Masou took his amulets with a solemn bow.

'Thank you, fair Ellie,' he said. 'We lack nothing but a rabbit and we would have a fine stew!'

He bent down and crept along the wall of the Great Hall so no one inside could see him. Then he took one of the torches that burned there and stepped forward through the broken doorway of the east wing. As we watched him, it seemed as if a cavernous hole was swallowing him up into the dark.

Ellie hung back. 'We shouldn't be doing this,' she whispered. Then she took a deep breath, held her elf-shot up like a shield and went in after him. ''Tain't right. 'Tain't proper!' I could hear her muttering.

Masou's torch lit our way very well as we went along an old passageway. There were chambers to the left, overlooking the moat, and further down, on our right, small glassless windows giving onto the main courtyard. It was strange to think that not long ago the east wing had been full of life. Now it was empty and silent. The builders had obviously been in and out, plundering glass and doors and other items for the new building. The spiders had been busy as well, for the torch-light flickered on huge cobwebs. It was not easy walking, as there were broken pieces of brick lying all over the floor. I found it particularly hard as Ellie was now clinging to my arm and I had the dogs on their leashes in the other hand!

It was very dusty, and every so often a strange draught whistled around us and tugged at our clothes. I told myself sternly that this was probably because there was no glass in the windows and was nothing to do with anything ghostly. The dogs trotted along, very quiet and well-behaved, worn out by their walk.

'The ledge is on the next floor,' I said. 'But where are the stairs?'

Masou's held up his torch and the light fell on the first steps of a spiral stone stairway at the far end of the passage. 'By my beard that shall grow one day,' he said, stroking his smooth chin, 'those stairs must be our path. With luck they may lead us to the ghost.'

'Then keep your voice down!' whispered Ellie.

At that moment there was a sudden, strong gust of wind and the torch flickered and went out. We all froze.

'God help us!' Ellie whimpered. 'We must leave this place.'

'We'll be all right,' I said, trying to convince myself as well as my friend. 'There is a little light from the moon. And we do not want to alert the ghost with our torch.'

'We do not want to alert the ghost at all!' hissed Ellie, trembling.

I decided that I must keep her busy, so I thrust the leashes at her. 'You hold onto the dogs,' I told her.

'I will, Grace,' said Ellie reluctantly. 'But they'd better be ready to run when I take to my heels!'

We went carefully on along the passage. Ellie refused to look right or left, but Masou and I glanced into each room as we passed. I must admit even I was getting anxious about what I might see. But every chamber was empty. Through the third doorway that we came to we could see the carved stonework of the oriel window lit up by the moonlight, but we did not linger.

We crept up the spiral staircase, listening out for any sound ahead of us. The dogs' claws made little clipping noises on the stone but that was the only thing we could hear. The passage above was much darker because there were no windows on the courtyard side, and only faint gleams of silvery moonlight trickling in on the other, where doorways opened off into chambers. It was certainly the right place for a ghost to walk. In spite of the heat of the summer evening I began to feel shivers down my spine. I marched forward as boldly as I dared. That is to say, I crept very slowly – but only because it was too dark to see where I was treading.

At last we came to a broken doorway and I peeked round it. I could see a large chamber with a long window. Indeed, the window was almost full length and had some bricks missing at the bottom, knocked out no doubt when the builders took the glass. Beyond it, lit up by the moonlight, was the ledge where the ghost had stood the night before!

'Quick,' I hissed. 'This is it! We must hide: if we are lucky the ghost will appear soon.'

'*Un*lucky more like!' muttered Ellie darkly.

By the light of the moon we could see a deep recess to the side of a broken fireplace. It was perfect for our purpose as it was full of shadow and there was room enough for all of us. Without a word I pointed to it and we all crept over and hid ourselves. Thankfully the dogs flopped down on the floor at our feet and went to sleep. We stood there in the dark, our backs against the wall, waiting. The moon shone an eerie light into the chamber.

Suddenly he was there! The ghostly figure of a man appeared in the doorway. He was pale as the grave, with wild hair and tattered clothes, just as we had seen last night. I watched in horrible fascination as he moved through the room to the window. Silently he stepped onto the ledge and stood there for what seemed an age, staring out over the moat. At last he turned very slowly and came back into the room. Then he stopped and gazed around. The moonlight was behind him so we could not see his face. But had he seen us? I shrank back into the shadows, and I could feel the others doing the same. I hardly dared breathe. I knew I was meant to be confronting the ghost, but at that moment I could not move a muscle!

At last the phantom walked towards the door and vanished. My heart was thumping loudly in my ears and my fingers were clenched so tightly that they hurt. I had just come face to face with a ghost! I shook myself. This was no time to be scared. I had come with the purpose of finding out why he haunted the east wing, and I was not going to give up now.

I slipped out from our hiding place. 'Quick!' I said urgently. 'We must follow him.'

'No we mustn't!' squeaked Ellie.

'Then stay here, sweet Ellie,' said Masou soothingly.

'Not on me own, I shan't,' Ellie replied, pulling at the dogs' leashes. They woke and trotted sleepily after us as we crept to the door. There was no sign of the ghost in the passageway outside, so we went on tiptoe to the top of the spiral stairs and I led the way down, peering round each bend in case he was waiting for us.

At the foot of the steps I was just in time to see the spectre enter the first chamber he came to in the passage. I was determined to confront this dreadful apparition and find out why he walks, though I confess that I was scared, and so I led my friends down the passage before I could change my mind.

When we reached the doorway I could sense Ellie hanging back.

'I'll hide here with the dogs,' she whispered in my ear.

'Stay with her,' I murmured to Masou.

Masou nodded and took Ellie's trembling hand reassuringly as I stepped through the doorway. The room was huge and the ghost was standing like a cold, grey statue in the very middle of the chamber, some distance from me.

'O ghost!' I called, and the words echoed horribly round the empty walls. 'Why do you haunt Medenham Manor? Why are you walking again?'

The spectre gave no answer. Instead he turned slowly to face me. I couldn't help but back away as two hollow eyes stared hard into mine.

'What is it that disturbs your peace?' I demanded again in a quivery voice. 'Speak, spirit. I know how you met your end.'

With horrifying slowness the ghost lifted a hand and pointed a finger straight at me. I felt as if a tiny piece of ice had slipped down my spine and my knees started to tremble.

'Move away, Grace!' shrieked Ellie from the doorway. 'He's putting a curse on you. Hold up your herbs!'

But I did not move, for I was staring at the ghost in fascination. Something about the way he moved seemed very human and not ghostly at all.

'He's got her under a spell!' I heard Ellie wail. 'Oh, Masou, she'll be lost to us for ever!'

The clouds covered the moon and the room fell into darkness. At that, the ghost turned away and walked towards the far wall, his hands held out before him. He vanished into the dark, and when the moon came out again, there was no sign of him. He seemed to have walked right through the wall!

Ellie rushed over to me. 'Speak to me, Grace!' she demanded. She dropped the dogs' leads, whipped out her sprig of basil and thrust it up my nose.

'I am all right, Ellie,' I insisted, backing away. 'The only danger I am in is from your amulet!'

'But that ghost cursed you!' Ellie insisted, trying to get near me with the basil again.

I held her off. 'No indeed,' I told her. 'I was just deep in thought. I am beginning to think that there was something not quite right about what we saw just now.'

'Something not right!' exclaimed Masou. 'By Shaitan, a truer observation I have never heard! We have just seen a phantom pass through stone!'

'And we're lucky it did nothing else!' snorted Ellie angrily. 'I told you we should never have come. Dabbling with the un-natural, 'tain't right! We shouldn't stay here a minute longer.' She picked up the dogs' leashes and led us from the room. Masou and I took one look at each other and followed.

'We still have no idea what troubles this ghost,' I sighed, as we burst out into the Knot Garden. 'And now I must go to the feast. But why would he not answer me?'

'Perhaps he is deaf,' suggested Masou. 'After all, he is more than a hundred years old!'

'Don't make mock,' said Ellie. 'He'll come after you – and serve you right.'

'Then I will need you to accompany me, fair Ellie,' said Masou. 'I am going to take the dogs back for Grace and you can fight off all spirits for me with your amulets.'

Ellie hit him with her basil, but I saw that she stuck close to his side as they hurried off with the dogs.

I hastened back to my chamber, where Fran was waiting for me on the orders of the Queen – which I thought very considerate of Her Majesty. I changed into my gown, dismissed Fran when she had done my sleeves and sat down with my daybooke. I was hungry enough to go straight to the feast, but I wanted to make this entry while it was still fresh in my mind. Though I am not like to forget a ghost walking through a wall, I still feel that there is something amiss with this spectre and wanted to omit no detail of the events.

Now I must hurry to the Great Hall. With luck there will still be some food left, for my stomach is growling like a bear now. Seeing a ghost has done wonders for my appetite!

On a window seat – very late

Once again I have been ousted from my bedchamber! I am on the window seat outside in the passage, for I know I shall get no peace to make my daybooke entry if I stay in there. The Maids are all in a terrible twitter after what has just happened in the Great Hall this evening. In truth, even I have to admit it is most exciting – although my ears have near been split by the shrieking of four Maids of Honour at once!

After I had finished writing my last entry, I hurried down to the Great Hall and made my curtsies to the Queen. Happily, it seemed I was not to starve after all, for there were a few sweetmeats and gooseberries in preserve. And there was some of Mrs Tiplady's cream and almond tart left too!

Mary Shelton laughed at the sight of me tucking into the delicious tart so heartily. 'Anyone would think you had not eaten for days, Grace!' she said. 'If you were so hungry, I warrant the Queen's dogs would have been content to wait until tomorrow for their walk.'

'The welfare of Her Majesty's dogs is much more important than my stomach!' I said piously between mouthfuls.

Mary Shelton simply stared and shook her head as if I had lost my wits.

As I ate, Carmina nudged Lady Jane and pointed to the far end of the table. 'What does Sir Thomas think he is wearing tonight?' She laughed.

We all looked at poor Sir Thomas Harrington, who obviously thought we were gazing in admiration, for he gallantly doffed his hat to us.

'He is never the smartest at Court,' said Lady Sarah, 'but tonight he has surpassed himself. Look at that doublet! It has lost all its stuffing!'

Most of the courtiers pride themselves on the bombast in their doublets, for they think it makes their chests look manly. However, Sir Thomas's sagged like an old turnip!

'Mayhap he dressed like that for a wager!' suggested Carmina.

'If I were him I would not wear such garb for a Queen's ransom!' sniffed Lady Jane scornfully. 'And he will have few admirers if he does not discard that dreadful cloak.'

They had a deal more to say on the subject. And as they looked down the table, Sir Thomas turned pinker and pinker with pride at all the attention he was receiving. It was as well that he could not hear what they were saying!

While they chattered on, I turned my mind to the problem of the ghost. I felt most unsettled, and it was not because I had come face to face with a spectre! It was something more than that. I started to think about the portrait of the first Earl and tried to picture him alive. Was the ghost really him?

My thoughts were interrupted by a snort from Carmina. 'And look at that fussy ruff up round his ears!' she cried.

Clearly she had not finished with poor Sir Thomas yet. I felt sorry for him, although I could not help but take a sneaky look at the offending ruff. The poor man had got it tied far too tightly. He has a short neck and it looked as if the ruff was propping his ears up! I thought he would have been better without one, but only very old people who give scant thought to fashion are ever seen without a ruff . . . And that was when the answer came to me!

The ruff! The ghost had been wearing a ruff. And I knew that he certainly should not have been. The first Earl had died a hundred years ago. No one had even heard of ruffs then, for there was no starch to make the folds stiff. Starch has only been used for the last five years.

How often have I heard Ellie raining curses on the person who invented the wretched stuff because it makes her hands so sore? A ghost from so long ago should not be wandering about in the latest fashion!

And then I remembered how the dogs had shown no signs of fear in the spectre's presence – though everyone knows that animals cower away from the supernatural – and I considered how human the ghost's movements had seemed to me. And I felt sure at that moment that the ghost was not a ghost at all, but a living impostor!

Yet one thing is certain: whoever is pretending to be the ghost must surely have some evil purpose in mind. At the very least he wishes to scare us witless, but at the worst Her Majesty's own life could be in danger. I realized I must speak to her alone, and without delay. But I could see that there was no chance of a private audience while she was sitting with her host and hostess.

'Whatever is the matter, Lady Grace?' asked Mary Shelton, as I fidgeted in my seat. 'You are most agitated. Has something disagreed with you? Shall I call Mrs Champernowne?'

Mrs Champernowne was the last person I needed! She would haul me away for some sort of nasty physic. 'No indeed,' I said in a rush. 'I, er, feel a little—' At that moment I heard a rumble of distant thunder, which gave me just the excuse I needed! 'I feel a little stuffy in the head,' I told her. 'I warrant it is because of the coming storm.'

I was saved from talking about the matter further, for Lord Reynold rose to his feet and took a deep breath. 'Your Most Gracious and Sovereign Majesty,' he began, 'I know not how to express the honour that your royal visit has bestowed upon my humble family.'

I sighed inwardly. My audience with Her Majesty would have to wait for quite a while; I could see we were set for a long speech. Although Lord Reynold claimed that he could not express himself adequately, he certainly tried for a good hour! He made the usual flatteries, which the Queen enjoyed enormously, and then he became emboldened by her smiles and compared her blessings on his house to practically everything he could think of, including the weather. It was a little unfortunate that as he made that particular likeness we could hear the storm outside drawing closer.

When he had at last run out of compliments for the Queen, he turned to the subject of the rebuilding of Medenham Manor. Lord Reynold praised his Master Builder, Mr Thompson, who was standing at the back of the hall. But when we all turned to acknowledge him and the Queen herself uttered a few words of praise, I noticed that Lord Reynold looked rather impatient. Mr Thompson seemed to hardly know where to put himself, he was so embarrassed by all the attention; he ended by nodding his thanks and bowing a great many times, until Lord Reynold broke in.

'Yes, yes,' he snapped at him. 'That will do!' And the poor Master Builder bowed some more and then backed out of the room, quite overcome!

His master proceeded to enumerate the remarkable features of the new building work

– all done in honour of the Queen, of course – and then to sing the praises of every builder and mason who has worked tirelessly on the rebuilding in order that Her Majesty could stay in 'the most modern house in Wiltshire'!

Just as I was wondering if he would mention each stonemason, carpenter and joiner by name, he came to an end and raised his glass to the Queen. As he did so, there was a sudden flash of lightning that made us all jump. Then an enormous gust of wind rushed through the hall and every torch went out.

We were left in pitch darkness.

The lightning flashed again and I could see that the Great Hall had broken into chaos. Some of the ladies were sobbing in fright, and no one seemed to know what to do – except for Lady Sarah who was suddenly next to Anthony Pemberton, one of her most faithful suitors. How she had found him in the dark I do not know!

'Bring lights!' someone ordered, and I could hear servants scurrying about in the dark trying to fetch torches.

At that moment there was a huge flash of lightning, a deafening crash of thunder and a bloodcurdling scream! I heard benches being knocked aside and goblets falling to the floor. Everyone began shouting at once.

'At the axe window!'

'The ghost!'

'It must be the first Earl!'

'And what is that upon the glass?'

'Blood! I believe it is blood!'

At the next flash of lightning, I saw it for myself. The axe window was indeed smeared with blood. And outside, in the angry storm, his hair flying and his eyes as black as night, stood the ghost!

Even though I believed the ghost to be a human impostor, I was startled. He had made himself look like a truly unearthly being. The lightning was coming so often now that for a few moments it turned the night into an eerie sort of day. With every flash we saw the spectre standing pale and motionless, staring in at us. Then he slowly raised one hand and pointed a bony finger at Lord Reynold!

At last servants ran in with torches. Now I could see amid the overturned benches and spilled drinks and sobbing Ladies-in-Waiting that Her Majesty was still seated calmly at the table. She is so brave – in the lightning the apparition had looked terrifying! My Lord of Leicester stood between her and the window, his hand upon the hilt of his sword, in order to protect her from any ghostly attacks. He is truly gallant.

Mr Hatton called for his Gentlemen of the Guard to go and drive away the ghost. But when the next flash of lightning came I saw that the ghost had vanished. I rushed over and peered through the glass, hoping I would see where he had gone. But all I could make out were the flaming torches of Mr Hatton's men as they searched among the bushes and trees and stared into the moat.

I took a candle and held it up to the blood-smeared glass of the window. What I saw froze me to the spot, for the blood spelled a single word: TRAITOR.

Lady Medenham and the other ladies were

being comforted, and all around I could hear a good deal of muttering about apparitions and curses and how terrible it was for such a good man as the Earl to be accused of being a traitor. Who on earth could he have betrayed?

Mr Hatton strode over to examine the writing on the window. It was smeared on the plain glass below the design of crossed axes. I was determined not to move until I had finished studying the ghost's message, and I think I got in Mr Hatton's way, but I would not be a very good Lady Pursuivant if I did not pay proper attention to such an important clue.

The letters were large and bold. But I noticed that they did not trickle, as letters in real blood would do. Instead they were thick and sticky and now I could see that the colour was not quite right. In fact, it looked more like lip paint.

And as soon as I realized that, of course I could guess where it had come from. When Lady Jane saw the ghost she had dropped her bag — and she had been most put out for it had contained her new lip paint! My heart began to beat faster. The impostor must have found the bag and then used the lip paint for the fake blood. Perhaps there were more clues on the window. I needed proof of villainy to take to Her Majesty. But there seemed to be nothing further.

Then I saw a tiny smudge of white further down the glass. It looked like the white lead that all the ladies of the Court put on their faces. And I guessed that this must be how the ghost makes himself look so pale. With enough white lead, anyone would look like a phantom! He has been very clever. I wonder how he contrived the rush of wind that blew the torches out – though mayhap that was mere chance.

At that moment the storm broke in earnest and it began to rain. The wind blew the water in torrents against the windowpanes. It beat against the glass so hard that it drowned out all other sounds and soon began to wash away the letters. As they trickled slowly down the glass, they could have been real blood.

I turned from the window. The ladies were still crying and wailing, and the gentlemen were having a difficult time calming them down. Indeed, some of those gentlemen who usually boast of their manly qualities seemed to have run away altogether! Lord Reynold was standing motionless in the middle of the Great Hall. He still had his goblet in his hand and he looked as pale as the apparition we had just seen.

Her Majesty rose from her seat. 'Clearly your new building work does not sit well with your ancestor, Medenham!' she declared coldly. And then she swept out of the room, closely followed by Mr Secretary Cecil and the Earl of Leicester.

I could see that Mrs Champernowne was trying to usher all the Maids of Honour away to their chambers. Unfortunately she had Carmina languishing on one arm and Lady Jane in complete disarray on the other. She could hardly move. Even Mary Shelton looked pale. I noticed that Lady Sarah still had her loyal escort and seemed to have recovered enough to smile and flutter her eyelashes at him.

'Grace!' panted Mrs Champernowne. 'You

are not to stay in this wicked room a moment longer. All the Maids must go to their chambers, look you – and without delay. Help Mary Shelton and come with us. You seem to be the only one who is capable of walking unaided. Lady Sarah, kindly request Mr Pemberton to lend you his arm for a little longer.'

I was desperate to stay and carry on investigating, but I could not think of an excuse, so I took Mary's trembling hand and followed. Mrs Champernowne prayed for deliverance from the wicked spirit and muttered curses on his head all the way up the staircase. Now that the immediate danger was over, Lady Sarah, Lady Jane and Carmina seemed to have lost some of their fear. Mrs Champernowne might tell them to hush until she was blue in the face but they would not be silent. They gasped excitedly about the spectre's eyes, his wild hair, his ghostly finger, and there was much talk of where the blood had come from.

'I warrant it was his own,' breathed Carmina with a shudder, as we reached the top of the stairs.

'I think not,' whispered Lady Jane. 'For spectres surely do not bleed. 'Tis my belief he killed some poor unsuspecting person and used the corpse's blood for his wicked message. To think I was in the garden with him. It could have been my blood!'

Lady Sarah squealed at this and clung ever more tightly to her young man's arm.

'I thank God *you* are safe, Lady Sarah,' he dared to join in. 'The evil spirit probably came upon an innocent soul in the depths of the nearby forest and slit his throat!'

There were fresh screams at this and Mrs Champernowne immediately sent the young man away for his gory talk.

As we walked along the passageway to our chambers I tried to puzzle out the impostor's purpose. For although I knew that none of the wild stories being told around me were true, I now felt certain that the villain meant ill to Lord Reynold.

His actions were going to put paid to all the building work, for who would be willing to work in a place that was haunted by an angry ghost? I wondered what the impostor had meant by his message on the axe window. Was he trying to make us believe that the first Earl considered Lord Reynold a traitor for pulling his old home down? It seemed likely, but since I was sure that the ghost was *not* the first Earl, I wondered what the impostor really had against Lord Reynold.

Lord Reynold seems to be such a jolly, good-natured soul; it is hard to believe that he has any enemy at all – especially one who would want to ruin his life. Yet I believe that that is what the impostor is trying to do, for Lord Reynold will certainly consider his life ruined if he falls out of favour with Her Majesty for bringing her to a haunted house!

As we reached our bedchambers Mrs Champernowne urged everyone to hasten to bed.

'I shall be instructing the servants to pack all your clothes early on the morrow,' she informed us, looking nervously around the walls as if the ghost might appear at any moment. 'Her Majesty will not stay in a house which is possessed by an evil spirit.'

I was sure she was right. The Queen had seemed very displeased. Poor Lord Reynold must be in despair. His high hopes for the royal visit and the future of his manor had been dashed by the ghost's spectacular appearance. I felt that it was up to me to solve this mystery. Yet how could I if we were to leave so soon? I decided to go to the Queen, tell her all I believed about the ghost being an impostor and beg her to stay a few days longer at Medenham Manor, to give me a chance to find the miscreant.

Mrs Champernowne finally stopped fussing around us and bustled off, telling us to get some sleep. But, of course, all the Maids were gabbling in high-pitched voices about the ghost. And they are all staying in our room again! I tried to tell first Mary Shelton and then Carmina that I was going to seek an audience with the Queen but no one was listening to me. So I gave up and slipped out quietly.

The Queen's quarters were in uproar when I arrived. The thunder was still rumbling in the distance outside, but that was nothing to the storm within Her Majesty's bedchamber.

Mr Secretary Cecil was at the Queen's side. 'My Liege,' he was saying solemnly, 'it is most assuredly the right thing to do. We shall be far from this accursed manor by noon. I cannot trust that you will be safe until then.'

The Queen seemed scarcely to be listening to him. 'Enough, sir!' she exclaimed. 'I have orders to give and not a Lady-in-Waiting to attend me.'

'I am sure they will be back soon, Your Majesty,' said Mr Secretary Cecil soothingly. 'They are already carrying out your previous instructions.'

'Then they are fools!' shouted the Queen, waving her comb at him. 'For now I have no one to tend to my hair!'

Mr Secretary Cecil bowed and backed away as I approached the Queen. I curtsied deeply and prayed she would not hit me on the head with the comb.

The Queen looked disapprovingly at me. 'Have you come to offer counsel, Grace, just as everyone else is trying to do?'

'No indeed, Your Majesty!' I assured her.

'Then you have more sense than the rest of them,' she sighed. 'Attend to my hair, if you will.' And with that, she thrust her comb into my hand.

It was my favourite of Her Majesty's combs, a lovely ivory one decorated with half moons of silver. I began to comb her beautiful red hair as soothingly as I could and said nothing for a few moments. I did not want to risk being ordered from her presence. The Queen can be very fiery when she is displeased, and I might have no further chance to speak with her until we were miles from Medenham Manor. It would be too late then.

I was wondering how I could have a private word with Her Majesty, when Lord Robert, the Earl of Leicester, came up and knelt before her. 'I would that Your Majesty had come directly to my home at Kenilworth instead of staying in this wretched manor for so long,' he said. 'I always felt the omens were bad here. You are not safe, and if any ill comes to you I shall—'

'I will not listen to your old woman's fussing, Lord Robert!' snapped the Queen. 'You need have no fear, for I do not intend any harm to come to my person. I have told you a thousand times that I am perfectly well guarded.'

'But, Your Majesty, what good are earthly guards against a visitation from another world?' protested Lord Robert. I know that he was overzealous because he loves the Queen so much, but at that moment he was only fuelling her anger.

'It is not I who will be in danger, my lord!' thundered the Queen, shaking a royal fist at him. 'It will be *you*, if you do not take good counsel and desist immediately from this nuisance. Now get you from my sight.'

Looking most displeased, Lord Robert bowed his way out with Mr Secretary Cecil and the Queen slumped back in her chair.

'Ah, Grace,' she sighed. 'I am weary of this matter! Lord Reynold assured me that despite the gossip there were no ghosts at Medenham.'

'Is a ghost necessarily a reason to leave?' I asked timidly.

To my relief the Queen gave me a smile. 'You and I may be made of strong resolve, Grace, but you were witness to the apparition's effect on the rest of the Court. I cannot have my Maids fainting at my feet and my Ladies-in-Waiting too frightened to venture from their rooms. Wherever a phantom walks there is much fear. We must leave.'

'Indeed, Your Majesty,' I said. Then I took a deep breath. 'Yet suppose that the ghost were not a spectre from beyond the grave, but some-thing altogether more earthly . . .'

The Queen frowned. 'My dear, you have grown fanciful with all the excitement of this evening!'

'My Liege, I trust that I have not!' I insisted daringly. 'On the contrary, I have good reason to think that our ghost is actually an impostor.'

'An impostor!' exclaimed the Queen, rising from her chair. 'Do you jest, girl?'

I stopped combing and told the Queen about the lip paint, the white lead on the window and the ruff worn by the ghost of a man who died one hundred years ago. I did not mention my two sightings of the ghost in the east wing, for I did not think she would express any pleasure at my night-time adventures!

'I believe he is nothing but a miscreant who wishes to frighten us all,' I finished, 'and spoil Lord Reynold's plans for his manor.'

The Queen sat down again, looking thoughtful. 'I believe you may have the right of it, Grace,' she said slowly. 'For what you have seen are not the marks of an *unearthly* visitation.' She took my hand in hers and patted it. 'I am proud of my Lady Pursuivant,' she told me, smiling, 'for it seems that no miscreant is too clever for you. While the whole Court loses its wits in fear, you keep a steady head on your shoulders.'

I smiled back. I feel so honoured when Her Majesty gives me praise.

'So, the ghost of Medenham Manor is no more spectral than I am,' she muttered. 'Poor Lord Reynold. I was too harsh with him in the Great Hall. But why should anyone wish him ill?'

'I beg Your Majesty to stay here just a few

days longer,' I pleaded, 'so that I may find the answer to that very question.'

The Queen held out her hand for me to remove her rings. She seemed lost in thought. 'Very well then, Grace,' she said at last. 'I know I can trust you to be discreet – but I can give you one day and no more. I shall tell the Court that I have changed my mind and we shall travel a day later. It would gladden my heart to help Lord Reynold if we can. He is a loyal subject indeed. And I shall order Mr Hatton to have his men search the estate thoroughly. There may yet be signs of this miscreant.' She looked hard at me. 'As for you, my lady, get you directly to bed now. You may begin your work on the morrow. But know this: I would not have you put yourself in any danger for this enterprise!'

'As ever, Your Majesty,' I said solemnly. But I had one more thing to ask. 'My Liege,' I said, 'may I request that we do not let it be known to the Court that the ghost is a mere impostor, for that may alert him and make him go to ground.'

'That is a good notion, Grace,' said the Queen. 'It shall remain a secret then. Now get yourself to bed.'

I curtsied my way to the door, and hesitated.

'What more do you want of me?' sighed Her Majesty.

'Nothing more, My Liege,' I assured her. 'I was merely wondering how you will keep the Earl of Leicester from having a seizure when you break the news that we are staying!'

The Queen threw back her head and roared with laughter.

When I reached my bedchamber I opened the door and entered without much thought. What a commotion! No one had noticed my absence and I believe the Maids must have thought me the ghost come to terrify them! I suppose it didn't help that opening the door so suddenly caused a draught that made the windows rattle violently and blew out the candle. It took a full ten minutes before they would quieten down, and that was only after I threatened to fetch Mrs Champernowne!

Only then could I come out here to the

window seat and write in my daybooke in peace. And now I must go to bed and try to sleep. Faith! I do not know when I have ever had such a short time to solve a mystery.

The Seventh Day of July, in the Year of Our Lord 1570

In the Great Hall

It is just after noon and we are having dinner. It is a lovely fresh summer's day after last night's storm. The sunlight is streaming in through Lord Reynold's windows and there is no trace of the ghost's words from yesterday. The north door is open so we can smell the scents from the Knot Garden coming in on the breeze. I have brought my daybooke to the table. No one is talking of the ghost, at least not in earshot of the Queen, but I wager all are wondering why we are still here at haunted Medenham Manor.

After breakfast this morning the Queen dismissed her Maids of Honour as Mr Secretary Cecil had a mountain of papers for her to sign. I was pleased, for it left me free to investigate – or so I thought. Unfortunately, before I could move an inch, Mrs Champernowne shepherded the Maids together.

'After all last night's excitements,' she said, leading us to the door, 'I think that a quiet morning of reading would not come amiss. Let us go to Lady Celia's chamber.'

I saw that I needed an excuse. 'My book is upstairs,' I said hurriedly. 'I will go and fetch it.' And I did not wait for Mrs Champernowne's reply, but darted away immediately. I had ten minutes, I surmised, before she would come looking for me.

The first person I needed to speak to was Lord Reynold. I wanted to ask him some more questions about the visitation last night. But our poor host was in such a nervous and distressed state that he had been confined to bed by his physician.

Next on my list was Ellie. She could gossip with the servants and perhaps learn whether there is anyone who holds a grudge against their master.

The clock in the courtyard was striking ten as I reached the passageway that led to our chambers. I hoped that Ellie would be making her rounds, collecting dirty bedlinen. Sure enough it was not long before a huge pile of sheets with a shabby kirtle and thin ankles beneath came tottering along the passage.

'Ellie Bunting,' I called in a serious voice. 'I have need of you. Come to my bedchamber this instant.'

Ellie's face appeared around the side of the pile and she winked at me. 'At once, your ladyship,' she said.

'What happened last night?' she gasped as soon as I had shut the door behind her and she had spilled her load onto the floor. 'I heard that a demon appeared at the window, breathing fire and cursing all within!' she exclaimed.

'Someone did come to the window,' I agreed. 'But it was no demon or spectre. It was just a man pretending to be a ghost. And it was the same man we saw in the old east wing.' I told Ellie all about the ruff. 'And I do not believe that a phantom could keep up with fashion!' I finished.

'You be right there, Grace,' chuckled Ellie, perching herself on Mary Shelton's bed. 'Not unless 'is tailor died along with 'im!' Then she scratched her head. 'Wait a minute. What about the message on the window, the one that was written in blood?'

'That was not blood,' I told her. 'It was merely commonplace lip paint.'

Ellie frowned. 'Don't forget,' she said, 'the ghost did walk through a wall. All three of us saw it.'

'I am sure there must be some explanation for that,' I said. 'Now, can you find out among the servants if Lord Reynold has any enemies or rivals? Anything you hear may prove useful.'

'All right,' Ellie agreed, 'I'll ask around.'

'Thank you,' I replied.

'By my life!' cried Ellie suddenly. 'I've just remembered. I did hear something about a jealousy! I was mixing the starch the other morning and Mrs Fadget was talking to Mrs Hollowbread. Well, Mrs Fadget was going on about how only she can starch the Queen's ruffs — although she would allow that the laundry here was well set out. And Mrs Hollowbread replied that it was indeed a fine laundry – a much better one than that at Sir Henry Fawley's house down the valley. And then she said that Sir Henry will be spitting feathers that Her Majesty decided to stay here and not at Fawley Hall!'

'Fawley?' I murmured. 'I have heard that name before, but where?'

'He's old and ugly and horrible to work for by all accounts,' Ellie said, wiping her nose on her sleeve. 'That's why none here will talk of the ghost. If they lose their jobs they will have to go to Sir Henry for employment.'

'Fawley!' I exclaimed, making poor Ellie start. 'In one of the stories the gravedigger told us, he mentioned that the first Earl had had a bitter enemy called Fawley. Mayhap there really is bad blood between the families. Thank you, Ellie. Now my investigation has some direction.'

I did not know Sir Henry Fawley, but I was certain he must be sometimes at Court. I wondered how far his jealousy of Lord

Reynold would allow him to go. Would he consider Lord Reynold a traitor for luring the Queen to his house? I had to find out whether he had been at the feast last night. If not, then it was possible that he was our ghost!

I helped Ellie fashion a carrying bag out of one of the sheets to make her burden easier, then I snatched up my reading book and left. I knew exactly who would be able to tell me all the gossip about courtiers!

The Maids were sitting with Mrs Champernowne and Lady Celia in a small parlour. They were having a quiet conversation when I burst in.

'Be seated, Grace,' said Mrs Champernowne straight away, 'and do not disturb us.'

I pushed my way between Lady Sarah and Lady Jane, who were sitting on a settle and having a fairly amicable chat – for them. Their books lay unopened on their laps. Lady Jane was now admitting that she had seen the spectre – and no doubt exaggerating the encounter! I tried to bring up the subject of Sir Henry Fawley, but she shushed me impatiently.

'The spectre stood there on the ledge,' she whispered to Sarah, 'and he threw back his head and let forth an unearthly scream. Then he shook his grizzled locks and stared right at me. His hand came up and he pointed with a trembling finger. "Beware, Jane," he said in a voice from the crypt. "Beware!" Then he rattled his chains.'

'What chains?' I asked, trying not to laugh.

'Long heavy chains draped all over his body,' she told us dramatically.

Carmina gasped. I tried not to giggle. This story owed more to Mr Bagshaw's imagination, I would wager, than what Lady Jane had actually seen.

'I cannot fathom why Her Majesty does not pack us all up and leave for Kenilworth,' said Lady Sarah, shaking her head. 'Who knows what the phantom will do next? I for one will not be getting a wink of sleep while we bide here.'

That made everyone stop and think, so I jumped in and asked about Sir Henry Fawley.

'Sir Henry Fawley?' repeated Lady Jane.

'Surely you have seen him at Court, Grace? And do you not remember talk of him at Windsor Castle before we came on progress? The Queen said she would visit Medenham Manor on the way to Kenilworth and Sir Henry begged her to go to Fawley Hall instead, but she refused. I believe the truth of the matter is that the Queen thought Fawley Hall would be too old-fashioned. It has not been updated for thirty years!' She shuddered in disdain.

'I do not think Her Majesty would mind that,' said Mary Shelton calmly. 'For her own palaces are old and yet she loves them. But since Lord Reynold is so favoured by Her Majesty, no doubt the Queen was eager to visit Medenham Manor and see the renovations for herself.'

So Sir Henry had reason to be jealous of Lord Reynold and might be wishing to spoil the Queen's visit. If that was so, then he had almost succeeded! He might even now be waiting for his moment to step forward and invite her to his house instead. Sir Henry would be sure to know that the ghost of the first Earl was said to have walked the manor a hundred years ago. How simple it would be for him to play the ghost and make it walk again!

But if he was the ghost then he could not have been at the feast. I had to find out.

'Was he at table last night?' I asked quickly.

Lady Jane looked down her nose at me. Ellie had said that Sir Henry Fawley was old and ugly so I suppose she could not imagine why I was interested in him.

'I do not recall seeing him,' said Mary Shelton thoughtfully.

'Nor I,' said Lady Sarah.

I sat bolt upright. Had I found my ghost?

'I saw him,' grumbled Carmina, fanning herself with her book, 'for I was stuck with him throughout the feast. And all he would talk of was building works. It was so vexing! I had Nicolas Bulmer on my other side and I would far rather have spoken to him. But no, Sir Henry must go on and on asking me questions about Medenham Manor and the new west wing.

When Lord Reynold gave his speech and spoke of the new building, I am sure Sir Henry was the only one among us that was truly interested!'

In that case Sir Henry Fawley himself could not be my ghost. But if he had a grudge against Lord Reynold he might have hired someone to do it for him.

'Do you think he is jealous of Lord Reynold's renovations?' I enquired casually.

'Jealous?' repeated Carmina, frowning. 'I think not. He could not stop saying how lovely it all is. He seems to want to copy everything Lord Reynold has done! It is bad enough hearing all about the manor from our host, let alone from his neighbour too.' She flicked open her book and then shut it again. 'If I had had to suffer any more of his talk of gargoyles and flying buttresses I believe I would have hit him with my goblet!'

So I do not think it is likely that Sir Henry had anything to do with the ghost. He did not sound jealous or bitter, and was probably guilty of nothing more than being a poor master with little inspiration for building works. I have to hope that Ellie has had better luck in finding something out.

The finger bowls are being brought round now so the meal is coming to an end. I must stow my daybooke in my bedchamber and continue my investigations.

Aha! One of the servants came in from the courtyard outside just now, and pushed the door open with his rear as his hands were full. The north door opposite was already open and I could suddenly feel quite a breeze blowing through from door to door. Other people must have felt it too, for some looked round as if they feared a visitation! I now have an inkling of how the ghost managed to make the torches go out. There was sure to be a door open last night as it was so hot and humid. All he had to do was open the opposite door as soon as there was a strong gust of wind. How simple – and yet, how clever!

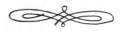

On a field near the manor

I have a lead at last! I cannot wait to follow it up, but I have to wait because now I must attend the Queen.

It is three of the clock and we are seated on a field to the side of the house near the Rose Garden. A makeshift Tilting Yard has been built here. Apparently Lord Reynold had planned to hold a joust long before the ghostly happenings and Her Majesty has persuaded him to continue with his plan. He is seated at her side. The poor man is very pale and shaky. He looks as if he should still be in bed, but he would not offend the Queen for all the world. My Lord Robert, the Earl of Leicester, has taken the Queen's favour and is to ride against Mr John Waldegrave, our host's brother. This joust is to be an entertainment and not to be taken seriously at all – except maybe by Lord Robert, who loves to show off his athletic prowess to his sovereign.

Lord Robert has excelled himself. His armour gleams in the sunshine, and he has a new shield with his family emblem of the bear and ragged staff. His black stallion is fully armoured as well and draped in bright cloth covered all over with the bear and staff. He outshines John Waldegrave – but Lord Robert always outshines everybody.

The two contenders have presented themselves to Her Majesty and ridden to either end of the tilting wall, lances held high.

Despite the fine show I am itching to sneak away. It is all I can do to sit still. I am writing in my daybooke to stop the fidgets.

After dinner I went to the kitchen to visit Mrs Tiplady again. The kitchen was a hubbub of activity. Some of the servants were sitting down at a table, eating their own dinner. Others were scrubbing at pots and wiping trenchers. I found Mrs Tiplady in a corner. She was rubbing wood ash onto some knives to clean them, but she jumped up and curtsied when she saw me.

'I would not disturb you, Mistress Tiplady,' I said quickly, 'but I had to come and tell you how much I enjoyed the cream and almond tart last night. Henceforth it will be my favourite, just as it was my mother's.'

Mrs Tiplady looked delighted. 'I am glad the Court is staying a while longer,' she said, taking up her knives again. 'I hope to persuade Lady Celia to let me make my Medenham Masterpiece for tonight.'

'What is that?' I asked.

''Tis mainly chicken and pounded pork,' she told me, 'but cunningly prepared so as it looks like a lizard!'

She began to explain how the chicken and pork is minced with herbs and fashioned into the shape of a lizard's head, body and tail, while behind us, two men were wiping and stacking trenchers. I do not think they knew I was there, for they soon began complaining about the building work.

'All that dust and noise,' said one. He had a gruff voice from too much pipe smoking. 'And to what end, I ask myself? There have been so many delays 'tis my belief it will never be finished.'

Mrs Tiplady was fashioning an imaginary dish on the table in front of her. 'We take four chicken legs,' she told me, 'and place two so, to look like the lizard's front legs. The other two go here to be the hind legs.'

Gruff Voice was still complaining and I had not intended to pay him much heed until I heard his next words.

'Of course, the ghost has seen to it that no more building will go on now!' he said.

I sat as still as I could at the mention of the ghost. I did not want the speaker to see me and stop talking. Happily, Mrs Tiplady had not yet finished with her description of the masterpiece.

'I use currants for the eyes and a red rose petal for the tongue. Then I cover the whole thing with artichoke leaves to look like scales and set it in a bed of lettuce so it appears to be crawling in the grass.'

'I would love to see it,' I murmured, straining my ears to hear the conversation behind me.

Gruff Voice's companion muttered something that I did not catch.

'Well,' declared Gruff Voice, 'Lord Reynold lost much time when he fell out with his Master Builder. You mark my words, that east wing will never be rebuilt.'

A falling out! So Lord Reynold and James Thompson had disagreed about the building work and the master builder felt aggrieved! I remembered when James Thompson was introduced to the Queen during our tour of the house. He had appeared to get on well enough with his employer then. But now I came to think of it, Lord Reynold had shown some impatience with him then – and again at the feast. I had not thought much of it at the time – assuming that old Lord Reynold simply wanted all the attention for himself – but now I wondered if there was more to it. And, I remembered with a thrill of excitement, James Thompson had left the feast shortly before the ghost made its appearance – how convenient!

Was it possible that Mr Thompson was just putting on a show of friendliness but was still secretly angry with Lord Reynold? Dressing up as a ghost and ruining Her Majesty's visit would be a perfect way to pay out a grudge! I resolved to find out more about Mr Thompson.

I suddenly realized that Mrs Tiplady was giving me a puzzled look. I'd been so busy with my mystery that I'd completely stopped listening to her!

'There's me gabbling on about food' – she laughed – 'while you're sitting there hungry, no doubt, though dinner was only an hour ago.'

She bustled round the table. 'Spinach pasties – just the thing. Now bide there while I fetch a cloth to put them in.'

I took the pasties gratefully, and left Mrs Tiplady parcelling up the last of the scraps and telling the spit boy to take them to the back door for any poor beggars who were waiting there.

I went in search of the Master Builder, and found him in the Knot Garden, where he had set up a trestle table near the east wing. The table was covered with papers and designs for the renovation.

'Good afternoon, Mr Thompson,' I called. 'It is a fine day after the storm, is it not?'

He looked up from his work, gave me a curt nod and then began some calculation or other. Well, he may not wish to exchange pleasantries with a Maid of Honour about the weather, but I was sure he would love to expound at length on his beloved building work.

'What is the next stage of the renovation, Mr Thompson?' I asked, trying to sound knowledgeable about such things. I would have mentioned flying buttresses if I had known what they were! I had no need. As soon as the Master Builder realized that here was someone who was interested in his project, he was delighted to talk to me.

'The east wing, here, must be demolished,' he said eagerly, showing me a complicated drawing. I put down my daybooke and pasties and leaned over the plans, nodding in what I hoped was a knowing way. 'We will then rebuild it, but five feet wider so that it is the same as the west wing. Symmetry is every-thing, my lady. It is the way of the future.'

'It sounds most . . . pleasant,' I said. 'Tell me, are these Lord Reynold's plans or your own?' I wished to see how he would react to hearing his patron's name.

'These are mine, I cannot deny,' he said proudly. 'But Lord Reynold gives much thought to my plans and then often comes forth with an excellent suggestion of his own. I count my blessings every day to have such a project and such a patron.' Then he frowned and shuffled his papers. 'I had hoped this manor would make my name in the world of archi-tecture, and perhaps gain Her Majesty's patronage, but now I am afraid it may not be.' He gazed sadly at the old east wing. This was my chance to mention the haunting and see how he reacted.

'Is that because of the ghost?' I asked, watching his face closely.

'Indeed, my lady,' he said straight away. 'And yet I cannot fathom why the first Earl would try to stop the renovation, for by all accounts he was as interested in new buildings as Lord Reynold himself. He built Medenham Manor after all, and I truly think he would have approved of the changes we are making! Alas' – he sighed heavily – 'if things go badly we may not be making any more such changes.'

The Master Builder seemed most disconsolate. If he was playing the ghost then he was a fine deceiver! He appeared to think so highly of Lord Reynold that it seemed unlikely there had ever been a disagreement between them, but I had to be certain.

'Forgive me, Mr Thompson, for repeating servants' talk,' I said boldly, 'but I heard that you and Lord Reynold had not always agreed about the building work . . .' I let my words tail off and held my breath, waiting for the master builder's response. Had I gone too far?

But Mr Thompson merely looked puzzled for a moment. Then his face cleared. 'You must have heard talk of George Colt,' he said, and I was relieved to hear that his tone was still friendly. 'He was the Master Builder here before me.'

'Another master builder!' I said, surprised. 'I believed this to have been *your* project, Mr Thompson. Where is Mr Colt? Why does he not work here still?'

'My friend George Colt started the project,' Mr Thompson explained. 'He was a fine master builder in his day, but he could only see his own vision and would not listen to other ideas. And that will never do. A master builder must always be open to the ideas of his employer, especially one as interested and knowledgeable as Lord Reynold. Lord Reynold was at his wits' end with George and in the end he dismissed him. He then came to me and I agreed to take on the project, but I was very sorry that George took it so hard. He told me we were no longer friends, you see.'

Mr Thompson had an honest manner and I felt sure he was telling the truth. But he had given me another suspect – George Colt.

'What a pity to lose a friend over it!' I exclaimed. 'What is Mr Colt doing now?'

'I have heard that he has not found any work since, my lady,' said Mr Thompson sadly.

'Folk have got to hear of his pigheadedness and refuse to employ him. He sits in the Boot Tavern in Medenham village most days, drowning his sorrows.'

I felt a great thrill of excitement for, suddenly, everything was beginning to make sense. If George Colt was the ghost, I reasoned, that would explain the word 'Traitor' on the window! Mr Colt might well think Lord Reynold a traitor for dismissing him and taking on another master builder in his stead. But although it was all quite possible, I could hardly go to Her Majesty and tell her to arrest Mr Colt just because he might *possibly* be the ghost. I needed some evidence that he was the miscreant, and that was going to be difficult to get in such a short time. The Queen has demanded answers by this evening or the whole Court will move on to Kenilworth.

I was about to take my leave when I noticed that Mr Thompson was obviously waiting for an answer to some question I had not heard. 'I am sorry,' I said quickly, 'but I was lost in contemplation of the, er, plans of the east wing.

How exactly will you demolish it? I am sure the hauntings will soon be over and the building work will continue.' But only if I can flush the ghost out, I thought to myself.

'I pray that you are right, my lady,' said Mr Thompson. 'We have planned to start by taking down the south wall at the front of the house.' He pointed at the place in his plans and launched into some very clever and very boring facts about demolition. As I gazed at the plan I suddenly realized what I was looking at. Mr Thompson's south wall was the very wall the ghost had walked through in front of Masou, Ellie and me! All my interest was now genuine and I looked more closely. I could see that there was something very strange about the plan.

'Why is the south wall much thicker than the others?' I asked.

'It is not odd to have one so thick in a house of this age,' Mr Thompson told me. 'Medenham Manor was built in the middle of the war between the Yorkists and the Lancastrians. Possibly the wall was built thus as a defensive measure.'

I suppose what he said made sense, but I felt it was significant that the ghost had disappeared there.

'Or it could have been a storeroom,' Mr Thompson added. 'They were sometimes built into the walls. But I doubt it, for we did not find any when we demolished the west wing.'

Without knowing it, Mr Thompson had given me the answer to the ghost's mysterious disappearance through the wall! I remembered that Ben Boggis, the gravedigger, had said that the first Earl had a secret chamber for his riches. I realized that the thick wall could conceal that very chamber! And it was not impossible that George Colt had discovered this for himself. He must have known the house well, for he had worked on it as Master Builder. Our ghost could have been using the hidden room to hide in before he made his appearances, and he might have left some evidence behind him. I was determined to have a look for myself. Hastily, I took my leave, snatched my daybooke and pasties from the trestle table and hurried off.

I wanted to search for the secret chamber at once but that was impossible. The Court was gathering for the joust and I had to come here and attend the Queen.

While I have been writing all this, Lord Robert has unseated poor Mr Waldegrave and is now being congratulated by the Queen. Everyone is watching them and I believe Her Majesty will say a few words. That will pass at least twenty minutes and then after that some Gentlemen of the Guard are going to give us a display of swordsmanship. This is my chance! I am going to hide my daybooke and pasties under my cushion – and pray that no one sits on them – while I sneak away to the east wing. I hope I will be back before I am missed.

Later

I am back! The Gentlemen of the Guard have not yet finished their display. The men of the Court are dazzled by the expert swordplay, while the ladies are dazzled by the dashing men wielding the swords. Consequently, no one noticed me slip back here to my seat.

I am desperate to tell Her Majesty what I have discovered, for it is truly amazing, but I cannot get her attention. So I have taken up my daybooke again. At least I can write down my news, even if I cannot tell anyone what it is!

No sooner had I sneaked away towards the east wing than I realized I could not go alone. Supposing the ghost was there, hiding in the secret chamber! If he meant me harm I would be defenceless. After all, he was a real person, and would likely use horribly real ways of silencing me! I decided to take Masou with me. I felt sure he would be only too willing to come, but I had no idea where he was.

As I went to look for him I came across Mr Somers's troupe practising on the grass beyond the Tilting Yard. At least, most of them were practising. Masou himself was lurking behind a tent. He had thrown down his juggling clubs and was listening to the Queen's words. Well, I think he was waiting for the swordplay to start really.

I could not get to him without being seen, so I hid behind a nearby tree and waited for him to turn round. Unfortunately for me he did not move, so in the end I was forced to throw twigs at him.

At last one hit him on the back of the head. He saw me and grinned, picked up his clubs and somersaulted his way over to me. Then he stood close by my hiding place and made a great show of his juggling practice.

'This is most strange,' he muttered out of the side of his mouth. 'I could have sworn that I saw a Maid of Honour disguised as a tree just now!'

'This is no time for jokes, Masou!' I hissed, keeping myself hidden from view. 'Can you come with me to the east wing? I think there may be a secret room there.' I told him what I had discovered about Mr Colt. 'So you see, it is not safe for me to go alone. I need your help,' I finished.

'Of course you do,' said Masou smugly, spinning the clubs ever higher. 'But tell me one
thing, my lady. Must I also disguise myself? If
so, you will have to wait while I uproot a bush
for the purpose.'

'Try not to act the buffoon, Masou!' I told
him with a smile. 'Just meet me at the back of
the east wing in a few minutes.'

'In that case I shall waste no time!' said the
gallant juggler, catching his clubs and laying
them in a pile. 'Let me find Ellie. Three would
be better than two. She is sure to come. Yet I
cannot be away for long. We are to perform a
masque at Kenilworth and I must practise.'

He did not appear to have been practising
very hard but I didn't say so!

I had only just arrived at the east wing when
I saw Ellie and Masou coming towards me. I
remembered the pasties and wished I could go
back and get them for Ellie, but there was no
time. Masou had a lighted torch, which looked
odd in the bright sunlight, but I realized it
would be useful in the gloomy ruins. Ellie was
carrying a stout stick.

'No amulets this time, Ellie?' I asked, winking at Masou.

'Masou has told me all about that Mr Colt, so I've got me trusty stick,' she said darkly. 'Just in case I need to clump 'im on the head!'

'Indeed.' Masou laughed. ''Twould make more of a bump than basil!'

Ellie ignored him and turned to me. 'Are you sure we have to go into that horrible place again, Grace?' she asked.

'Yes, Ellie,' I said. 'I am afraid we do. Now if I am right, and there is a secret room in there, we may be on our way to solving this mystery. Anyway, look on the bright side: at least we need not fear a ghost this time.'

'Grace is right,' said Masou solemnly. 'We need not fear a ghost. We have only to deal with a living villain, who may simply want to tie us up or throw us in the moat or—'

'Don't you try and scare me, Masou!' warned Ellie, waving her stick at him. 'Else I'll do some practising on you!'

'Enough.' I grinned. 'We are perfectly safe. No one will dare come near us if Ellie wields her stick! But we are delaying. Let us go.'

We entered the east wing by the old doorway at the back and picked our way over the broken bricks along the passageway. We came to the big, gloomy chamber where we had watched the apparition vanish. Masou strode over to the wall and held up the torch.

'Here is the very place where our ghost disappeared,' he said, examining the spot. 'And yet I can find no door – even a disguised one – through which he could have gone. All is solid wall!'

'Mayhap he *was* a spectre!' quavered Ellie, glancing about her fearfully.

'Now you know he cannot be, Ellie,' I said quickly, before Masou could make one of his jokes. I took her by the hand. 'Come, let us see if there are any clues as to how the impostor disappeared so expertly.'

We joined Masou by the wall and bent to examine the stonework. There were rusting candle sconces at intervals along the wall. But we could find not the faintest sign of any doorway.

I was determined not to give up. 'I have an idea,' I said. 'Masou, I will need you to pretend to be the ghost.'

'Whatever your ladyship wishes!' exclaimed Masou with a bow. He put the torch into my hand, then made his eyes wide and wild and began to stagger towards us as if sleepwalking. He looked so comical that even Ellie chuckled a little.

'No.' I laughed. 'I meant you to walk exactly in the footsteps of our spectre, and see if we can get to the truth that way.'

'Then you should have said so' – Masou shrugged – 'although I confess I cannot see a good reason for such play-acting.' He went obediently to the middle of the room, where we had seen the ghost standing, and walked slowly towards the wall.

When he reached it he put out his hands as if to feel his way through the stone.

But as he touched the wall, it moved! Ellie gasped and Masou jumped back with an oath.

I dashed to the wall, and now I could see what had happened. A slab, taller than a man, had been set into the wall on a pivot, so that when it was pushed the whole slab swung smoothly like a door to reveal an opening. And yet when it was shut, there was no sign of a door at all!

'So now we know how our ghost seemed to walk through a wall,' I said. 'Most clever!'

I held the torch towards the opening to see what was beyond. And Ellie and Masou gathered to peer over my shoulder.

'Let us leave this place, Grace,' Masou muttered suddenly. 'There may be something evil yonder. I have a feeling that chills my blood.'

'Stow it, Masou!' said Ellie, probably thinking he was joking. 'I've told you I'll whack you if you try to scare me again.'

But I looked at Masou's face for signs of a smile, and saw that his expression was serious. I felt a shiver of fear. This was not like Masou. We knew there was no ghost and yet something was troubling him: he was not being his usual bold self. What could be in the chamber beyond?

I took a deep breath. 'Come on,' I said, stepping forward. 'We must go in.'

Ellie followed me into the little room and Masou came reluctantly behind. I held the torch high to examine the ghost's hiding place. But what I saw made me gasp in horror. Ellie let out a piercing scream and stumbled backwards out of the secret chamber, while Masou made a hurried sign with his hand to ward off evil spirits.

There in the far corner, sitting on the floor with its back against the wall, was a skeleton. Its bony white hands lay at its sides and its jaw hung open in a ghastly grin. It still wore the ragged remains of clothes from a bygone time, and it was truly a gruesome sight.

Hanging loosely from one finger was a ring. And on it I saw the Medenham crest.

'The gravedigger's tale must have been true!' I gasped. 'These are surely the bones of the first Earl of Medenham. He was indeed walled up and left to starve by his own son!' I shuddered at the thought of such a horrible, slow death.

Then a faint smudge of white on the floor caught my eye. I bent down and touched it with my finger. It was white lead, just like the tiny smear I had seen on the axe window. And a horrible thought entered my brain. 'This must be where our impostor transforms himself into a ghost!' I said in disgust. 'How horrible to think he is willing to share the chamber with a long-dead corpse and, worse still, pretend to be the ghost of the poor man whose body lies here unburied!'

'What an evil man he must be!' exclaimed Masou. 'And hell-bent on ruining Lord Medenham.'

'Let us go,' I urged, turning away. 'For the miscreant may yet be near. I, for one, have no wish to encounter him in this place.'

'Me neither!' agreed Ellie, grasping my hand and hauling me back through the opening in the wall. 'Shut that skeleton in again and let it be.'

Masou pulled the door back into its place, using the candle sconce as a handle. Now it looked just like the rest of the wall.

'We cannot simply let it be, Ellie,' I said. 'The remains of the first Earl must be laid to rest properly. It is all we can do for the poor man now. I will make haste and tell this news to the Queen.'

And now I am sitting here, wishing the swordplay would finish so that I can speak to Her Majesty!

Early evening, in the Rose Garden

I am sitting under an arbour in the Rose Garden to catch up with my daybooke before supper.

The Queen finally saw my desperate efforts to be noticed from my seat at the joust, so I went and knelt before her.

'Lady Grace!' she said sternly. 'I have no doubt that your grimaces spring from your pleasure at this display, but I would counsel you to keep them to yourself before you frighten us all off!'

'I humbly beg Your Majesty's pardon,' I murmured, bowing my head. 'But I have just found something that has banished a certain *spectre* from my mind and lifted my *spirit*. It will surely gladden all our hearts, especially that of our host.' I could not speak directly for fear that others might overhear and find out my secret work in the service of the Queen, but Her Majesty looked sharply at me and I knew she understood.

She rose and took me aside. 'Speak, Grace,' she said in a low voice. 'Tell me this news without delay.'

I described to her what I had found in the east wing and Her Majesty looked shocked but recovered herself quickly. She wanted to know every detail of where the bones were to be found.

'You have done exceedingly well, my Lady Pursuivant,' she said. 'I am sorry that Lord Reynold will never know his true saviour, but the secret of your service to me must be kept. I will have to tell the news without mention of your name. Then I shall give orders that the bones be buried in holy ground.'

'But what of the impostor, Your Majesty?'

I urged. 'He may still bear a grudge against Lord Reynold.' I was about to tell her that I thought I knew who he was, but she gave me no chance.

'He will be unable to trouble us once he knows that the bones will be laid to rest with all ceremony,' she said firmly, 'for there will be no excuse for a ghost to walk. And if this villain's intention is to discredit Lord Reynold and stop the building work, then he has failed. Lord Reynold's plans for his magnificent estate will come to fruition.' She took my hand. 'Now, Grace, come back to the display and I shall make the announcement. I am very grateful to you that we may continue our stay at Medenham Manor.' And with that Her Majesty returned to her seat and spoke a few words to Lord Reynold. He gave orders that the display be stopped and the Queen rose to address us. There was an immediate hush.

'My lord,' she said in that tone of voice she uses when she has something of particular import to announce. 'We have good tidings. We set some of our men to find out more about the ghost that troubles us here. They have been most diligent.' Here she gave me a brief glance that made me feel warm inside. 'They have found the cause of the spirit's distress. The remains of your ancestor, the first Earl of Medenham, have been discovered here at the manor.'

Lord Reynold gasped and held his wife's arm for support.

'We need fear this ghost no more,' declared the Queen, 'for its bones shall be buried in the churchyard and thereafter rest in peace.'

There was an excited murmuring in the watching crowd and the Gentlemen of the Guard all looked at each other, rather puzzled, wondering no doubt which of them had made this discovery.

Lord Reynold went paler than ever. It was as if he hardly dared believe the good news. 'Your Majesty,' he said feebly, 'I truly thought that the first Earl died far from here. May I ask where the bones were found?'

'They lie walled up in the old east wing,' said the Queen. There were muffled cries of surprise all about us. 'Come, we shall show you without delay.'

Leaning on his wife's arm, Lord Reynold walked beside the Queen to the east wing. The whole Court followed behind. Nobody wanted to miss the excitement!

When Lady Celia saw the rough floor that the royal shoes were about to tread upon, she immediately gave orders that the way be cleared and cloth be brought for Her Majesty to walk on. When it was laid down to our hostess's satisfaction we followed the Gentlemen of the Guard down the passageway into the chamber.

As we all stood and stared at the wall with the hidden door, I realized that there was one important thing I had not told Her Majesty. Everyone was waiting for her to reveal the secret of the room beyond, and she had no idea how to find it!

Of course, I could not show her in front of everyone, for that would prove I knew more than I was meant to! There was only one thing for it: I would have to play the ham-fisted

Maid. (No one would be surprised, as I have the reputation of being clumsy – very unfairly in my opinion!) I decided I would step forward, pretend to trip and fall against the secret door. First I made sure that I was in the right place. Then I stretched out my hands and lunged forwards with a silly squeal. As I hit it, the hidden door swung open and I fell onto my knees in the room beyond. Behind me I could hear gasps and cries of surprise.

Mrs Champernowne elbowed her way forwards and helped me to my feet. 'What are you thinking of, Grace?' she scolded. 'There's enough going on here without your silliness, look you.'

I muttered an apology and bobbed a quick curtsy to Her Majesty. I saw that the Queen's eyes were twinkling and she gave me a grateful smile.

Lord Reynold called for a torch. Then he took it and ventured cautiously into the secret chamber. He stared at his ancestor's remains without a word. Then he stepped forward and took the ring from the bony finger. 'So my ancestor was indeed walled up and left to die!' he murmured, gazing at the ring. 'I had always discounted such stories, for they seemed too awful to be true.' He gave a sorrowful shake of his head. 'And yet I must now believe that the second Earl truly did murder his own father!' He knelt at the Queen's feet and I could see that there were tears in his eyes. 'Your Majesty,' he said brokenly. 'How can I ever repay you for your gracious help this day?'

'Your bountiful hospitality is payment enough, my lord,' the Queen assured him gently. 'In truth, I am as relieved as you that this matter is at an end.' She held out her hand and raised the poor man to his feet. Then she gave his hand to his wife and clasped their hands together as she addressed us all. 'Be sure of this. The name of Medenham is in no way besmirched by the folly of an ancestor. We know our lord and his lady to be most true and loyal servants of the Crown. And we will be happy to stay as long as we first intended.'

The Queen turned to Lord Reynold. 'Come, my lord,' she said. 'We must order a Coroner's Court to convene. As soon as they have released the body and given permission for us to proceed, we shall make preparation for the burial of these sad bones. At last the unhappy ghost shall be laid to rest.'

There was talk all around as we followed the Queen and Lord Reynold out of the east wing and back towards the Great Hall. I walked along with the other Maids of Honour and listened to their chatter.

'For my part I am glad that all is now well for our host,' said Mary Shelton, smiling. 'Olwen's mother's cousin is one of Lord Reynold's joiners, and she told me that the instant the builders heard about the appearances of the ghost they put down their tools and refused to work a moment longer in a haunted house. Now it is to be hoped they will come back.'

'I am most relieved too,' agreed Carmina. 'Though I was never much frightened by the ghost.'

I could scarcely help exclaiming at this. Carmina had let out the loudest screams of all over the last few days!

'I wonder which Gentleman of the Guard found the skeleton,' said Lady Sarah, looking around admiringly. 'I should not like to have been in his shoes when he did!'

'Unless you had the arms of Anthony Pemberton to faint into!' replied Lady Jane a little acidly. I think she was rather put out that, when it came to gentlemanly protection, Lady Sarah had done better out of our ghost's visits than she had.

'Grace may know something!' said Carmina, before Lady Sarah could give a sharp answer. 'You were with Her Majesty just before she made her announcement, were you not?'

'Indeed I was, but in truth—' I began.

'Did she divulge anything to you?' demanded Lady Sarah eagerly.

'I doubt anyone would believe that the Queen confides in Grace over such important matters!' said Lady Jane with a dismissive shake of her head.

I opened my mouth to protest, then remembered just in time that this was what everyone must believe, if my office as Queen's Lady Pursuivant is to remain a secret.

'You are right, Lady Jane,' I told her humbly. 'The Queen told me nothing of the find at all.' This was quite true, for it was I who had told her!

They went on chattering about the news on the bridge, across the courtyard and all the way to the Great Hall, where refreshments had been set out. I followed, lost in thought. But it was hard to concentrate with all the hubbub about me, so I went back to the Tilting Yard, fetched my daybooke from under the cushion and came here to the Rose Garden. (The pasties were sadly squashed beyond all hope so I threw them to the carp in the moat.)

Somehow, I do not feel any of the pleasure that the solving of a mystery usually brings. True, I have found out why the first Earl disappeared, and I am very glad that he can now be given a decent burial. But I have not been able to prove to everyone that the ghost was just an impostor, nor have I finally discovered who that impostor was. And now that the body is to be laid to rest, the miscreant cannot continue to walk as the ghost. I want this man brought to justice, but I know not how I can unmask him.

The Eighth Day of July, in the Year of Our Lord 1570

In the orchard

I am sitting in the orchard on a grass seat under some apple trees. It is near to two of the clock in the afternoon and the sun is very hot. I have to be careful for there are some lazy bees flying about between their hives.

I am not feeling lazy in the least. I have something of great import to tell the Queen but she is closeted with Mr Secretary Cecil, so I am using the time to write in my day-booke once again.

Mrs Champernowne woke us this morning with some good news. The first Earl was to be buried in the family vault today, and Lord Reynold had asked for the whole household and everyone in the village to attend the funeral. As soon as I heard this my heart leaped; I felt sure George Colt would be among the mourners. I resolved to try and find him there.

The Coroner wasted no time in releasing the remains – he would not dare when Her Majesty ordered it so – and the funeral was at ten of the clock. We all gathered in the main courtyard. The first Earl's coffin had been placed on a bier of slatted wood and covered with cloth bearing the Waldegrave family arms. Six Gentlemen of the Guard were to carry the bier on their shoulders to the church.

Her Majesty and Lord Reynold led the procession. The Queen wore a mourning mantle of purple velvet, as befitted the funeral of an earl. Her Council of close advisers, the Ladies-in-Waiting and the Maids of Honour followed. Lady Celia and the rest of the Court and servants walked behind. We all wore our darkest colours. Then came the Gentlemen of the Guard bearing the coffin, and following them, forty-three villagers clad in black cloaks, one for each year of the Earl's life. We progressed slowly.

Master Peabody and the other villagers were at the lychgate, waiting to receive the

Earl. To one side of the churchyard, tables had been set up. Lord Reynold had ordered a funeral feast to be held for all the villagers after the ceremony.

As we followed the coffin through the churchyard to the family vault, I looked around, wondering whether George Colt was among the sea of faces. Then I spotted old Ben Boggis. I lingered as everybody gathered round the vault and took the opportunity to have a word with him.

'Good day, Ben Boggis.' I smiled. 'Now everyone knows that your story of the first Earl was the true one.'

'Yes indeed, my lady,' replied the grave-digger, doffing his hat. 'I'm glad the poor soul will have a proper burial at last and be laid with his wife and family.'

'And the whole village has come to see it done,' I said.

I wondered how I could ask if George Colt was there. It would seem a strange question. I could think of no subterfuge so I decided to be direct.

'Tell me,' I said, 'I have heard talk that Lord Reynold used a master builder before James Thompson. Is that man here?'

'You mean George Colt,' replied the old gravedigger. 'I certainly have seen his face today.' He squinted in the sun and scanned the crowd. 'There he stands, by the lychgate. He's keeping out of Lord Reynold's way, I'll be bound. There's no love lost between those two.'

I looked over to the lychgate and saw a man in a blue velvet doublet and hat leaning against the churchyard wall. His face was solemn, but that is no more than you would expect at a funeral. I did note, however, that although his clothes had been fine once, they were not well cared for and his beard needed a trim.

'He don't seem to do much building nowadays,' snorted Ben Boggis, 'for he spends most of his time at the Boot Tavern! He still bides in the village but he's lost his fine house and had to move to a smaller one. And he don't have the good name he once did.'

I could see Mary Shelton beckoning to me so I said goodbye to the old man and made my way to the vault. The coffin was now resting on trestles. Above our heads the church bell rang out to announce that the funeral was about to begin. Master Peabody glanced nervously at Her Majesty, who nodded at him to start.

' *"I am the resurrection and the life," saith the Lord,*' he intoned.

It was very still in the churchyard. The sun had gone behind a cloud and I could not hear any birds singing. I do not like funerals, for I remember my mother and feel very sad. I tried instead to think about the first Earl and hoped he would now rest in peace and dignity.

Master Peabody paused in his words and nodded to the six Gentlemen of the Guard. They lifted the coffin and carried it down into the vault as the priest spoke the final words of the service.

' *We therefore commit his body to the ground; earth to earth, ashes to ashes, dust to dust; in the sure and certain hope of the resurrection to eternal life,*' finished the priest.

The church bell rang out again and the

service was over. I looked round for George Colt. The first Earl might have been buried but my investigation was not over. I still had a ghost to catch!

I spotted him still standing by the lychgate and quickly made my way over there, treading on a few toes in my haste! But I was too late, and he was well down the path to the village by the time I reached the gate. I wanted to follow him, but a Maid of Honour could not go into the village alone. And then I spied Ellie, who was trying to dodge Mrs Fadget. I had not noticed her before, for she was wearing a different kirtle — less shabby than her own. I grabbed her hand and pulled her along as I tried to keep Mr Colt in sight.

'I must speak to that man,' I explained as we hurried after him, 'and you must be my servant.'

'I'll be glad to play your servant,' said Ellie, her eyes bright with the adventure. 'For all that waits for me back at the manor is a vat of chemises, and they'll keep. And I certainly look the part today, for Mrs Twiste lent me this old kirtle of hers especially for the funeral. I have to give it back after though,' she added regretfully.

We followed Mr Colt down the road into the heart of the village. Then he turned into a smaller street and stopped at the door to a roughly thatched cottage. He opened it and stepped inside.

'That must be where he lives,' I whispered. 'Come on.'

'What are we going to do?' asked Ellie in excitement.

'We're going to visit him,' I told her. 'And I hope to find proof that he really *is* the ghost – if he is hiding his costume and white lead in his house. We must have an excuse, however.' I thought for a moment. 'I know! I will claim that I am in need of some building work.'

We reached the cottage. It was a small dwelling and spoke of a man down on his luck. One of the shutters was hanging by a hinge and the glass in the only window was smeared and dirty.

I knocked boldly on the door. Mr Colt opened it and for a moment he looked most shocked. I am sure he recognized me from our late-night encounter! I had not thought of this when I grabbed Ellie's hand and followed him. I realized I must quickly make it clear that I had no notion he was the ghost and had come with quite another purpose.

'Mr Colt?' I enquired, trying to sound grown up and important and nothing like the quivering girl who had confronted him in the old east wing. 'I am Lady Grace Cavendish, Maid of Honour to Her Noble Majesty, Queen Elizabeth, and I am in need of a master builder.'

'Yes, my lady.' Mr Colt said, bowing deeply and looking immensely relieved. His doublet was undone at the neck and he hastily fastened the buttons. 'How can I be of service?'

'I am newly come into some property,' I went on. 'It lies in the next county and is in need of much renovation. An elderly uncle lived there for years and did nothing to the place.'

'You are most welcome, my lady,' gushed

Mr Colt, eager now that he thought some work was coming his way. 'Please enter my humble abode. Of course, er, this is not my regular house. My own is much bigger. I am simply having that improved, just as you yourself are intending.'

George Colt was a good play-actor. If I had not known he was lying, I would have been convinced by his words. He led us into a dark parlour and offered us a seat. I stared hard at him to see if I could recognize him as the ghost, but I could not be certain.

'May I fetch you some refreshment, my lady?' simpered our host. 'Some mead perhaps?'

'Yes please,' I said, hoping I sounded gracious. I needed to prolong the visit until I had found out something of use.

He scuttled into a back room and we could hear the sound of glasses being hurriedly washed.

I looked around the small chamber. It was sparsely furnished. Apart from the rickety table at which we were seated, there was only a settle against one wall and a chest under the window. On the chest was a wooden box, its lid covered by an embroidered cloth. Another doorway led to a single bedchamber. From what I could see that room was empty but for a palliasse on the floor. There did not seem to be many places where George Colt could have hidden the devices he needed for his ghostly performances.

He returned with some glasses of mead. Ellie drank hers quickly. This was a rare treat for her.

'How large is your inherited estate, Lady Grace?' Mr Colt asked.

Hell's teeth! I had not thought far enough ahead. He was waiting for me to describe my mythical mansion! I did not want to waste time on that.

'I do have some questions of my own, Mr Colt,' I said, 'before we get down to dimensions.'

He nodded eagerly.

I decided to start with a compliment. 'I am an admirer of your work,' I said, 'but I did hear that you had some trouble with your last project at Medenham Manor.'

The builder's face darkened. 'I would not call it trouble!' he said quickly. 'And it is all in the past – water under the bridge. It was a mere difference in ideas about design and all was quite amicable.' Mr Colt sounded sincere but his eyes would not hold mine. They darted around the room as he spoke, and I noticed that more than once they came to rest on the wooden box atop the chest. 'Why, only today I saw Lord Reynold at the church,' he went on, shuffling his feet a little.

Mr Colt may well have *seen* Lord Reynold, I thought, but that was all.

'And what good news for all those at the manor to have the first Earl discovered and laid to rest at last!' George Colt was saying in a hearty tone that sounded forced to my ears.

I realized that my quarry was trying to evade the subject of his differences with Lord Reynold. Of course, no master builder who is trying to get a new commission would want to mention problems with a former employer, so that was quite natural. But I was becoming more and more sure that he had been the ghost, and as we talked I noticed that he could not stop his eyes from returning nervously to the box on the chest — and that made me wonder what was inside.

I picked up my glass and drank down the mead. 'Delicious,' I said. 'Could I trouble you for some more, Mr Colt?'

I was pleased with that, for our host had no option but to go off and fetch some. The moment he had gone, I leaped up and made for the box. Ellie looked at me curiously.

I carefully moved the cloth — taking care to remember exactly how it had lain — and then I lifted the lid. Immediately I felt a rush of despair — the box was empty!

I stared at it in disappointment. I had been so sure that here I would find some evidence. Then I saw that the inside of the box looked much shallower than its outside. Could there be a secret compartment at the bottom? I felt about with my fingers and at last found a small loop of thread. I pulled it and the bottom lifted: I had been right! There was a hidden compartment — and in it I could just make out

Lady Jane's bag and her pot of red lip paint!

Now I was convinced that George Colt was the ghost. However, I knew that if the Gentlemen of the Guard were sent to arrest him, he might get wind of it and get rid of the lip paint. Besides, how could I prove he had used the lip paint to write TRAITOR on the window? The rain had washed the incriminating letters away, and there was nothing else that pointed to George Colt being the phantom.

But I was afraid to let the matter rest. Mr Colt was sly and clever, and even though he could not play the ghost any more, I did not doubt he would find some other way to ruin Lord Reynold's good name.

I knew that the most certain means of proving George Colt's guilt was to catch him in the garb of the ghost. Yet how could that be done? I thought hard. All at once an idea burst into my head like a firework. I would get him to play the spectre in front of the whole Court one last time. And I would make sure Mr Hatton's men were ready to arrest him when he did.

Suddenly Ellie gasped and I heard Mr Colt coming back. I hastily closed the box and picked up the cloth, but there was no time to put it back.

'My lady,' said Mr Colt sharply, 'what are you doing?' I turned to face him, cloth in hand. He looked very angry. I had to find an excuse for my actions or Ellie and I could be in danger.

'Forgive me, Mr Colt,' I said calmly. 'I could not resist having a closer look at this fine piece of cloth. The couching and the split stitches are exquisite.' I was lying. It was a poor piece of embroidery. Indeed, I had no idea if the thing in the centre was meant to be a dog or a duck! But I was counting on the fact that Mr Colt would not be an expert in needle-craft. 'I was just saying how fine it was to my servant, was I not, Ellie?'

Ellie nodded so hard I thought her head would fall off. 'Yes, my lady,' she squeaked.

Mr Colt looked suspiciously at me, then at the box.

'Now,' I said brightly, putting the cloth carefully back and taking the mead from him, 'about the huge and expensive changes to my house . . .'

Reminded of the possible commission, Mr Colt became all smiles again. He must have believed my story, and I felt my knees sag with relief. I quickly sat back down with Ellie, who was looking very pale and worried. She gulped her mead down in one go, then jumped to her feet.

'Begging your pardon, my lady,' she said with a curtsy, 'but you will remember that Her Majesty the Queen expects you at the funeral feast back at the manor.'

Clever Ellie! I had been wondering how to get us away!

'In truth you are right, Ellie,' I said, jumping up beside her as if I had sat on hot ashes. 'Forgive me, Mr Colt – I had forgotten and I must not keep Her Majesty waiting. As for you, are you not joining the feast laid out for the villagers? You have been so closely con-nected with the manor and I am keeping you from the funeral fare!'

Mr Colt looked down at his feet. 'I am too

busy with my many commissions,' he mumbled. 'But not too busy to do work for you, my lady!' he added in a rush.

'I am glad of it.' I smiled. 'I shall return on the morrow to continue our talk.'

'I will await you, my lady,' said Mr Colt. 'You will perhaps mention that you have been discussing business with me?' He seemed very impressed that I was so close to the Queen and I imagine he thought he might get even better commissions than I could offer.

I smiled as if in agreement. I felt no pang of guilt, for I believed him to have done Lord Reynold and his family great wrong. But I had one more task to perform: I had to set the trap for our ghost.

We were just stepping into the street when I turned to Mr Colt as if I had suddenly remembered something. 'Perhaps we will see you tonight at Medenham Manor?' I said sweetly, as if it was an afterthought. 'There is to be a grand event there.' I knew he was probably the last person Lord Reynold would invite but I acted as if I had no notion of that. 'Her

Majesty's troupe is to perform a splendid masque in front of the east wing. And, of course, now that the bones of the first Earl have been laid to rest there is no fear of his ghost appearing!' I gave a shiver. 'At least, I hope we shall see no ghosts,' I went on, 'for if burying the first Earl does not stop him haunting the manor, then Lord Reynold is surely doomed!' I made sure that my face looked solemn at this, and I shook my head sadly while all the time watching to see if my words were having the desired effect. I saw a brief look of triumph pass over George Colt's face. It was enough! My trap had been set. I swept off, with Ellie hurrying after me, open-mouthed.

As soon as we were out of sight, she grabbed my arm. 'What were you on about, Grace?' she asked. 'There's no masque planned for tonight, else Masou would have told me.'

'I know,' I groaned. 'It was all I could think of to lure Mr Colt to the manor as the ghost once more. The troupe have been practising a masque to be performed at Kenilworth. I think they will be able to bring the performance forward, but that is only if I can persuade the Queen to command it! If George Colt hears there is no masque he will not come.'

'Course 'e won't!' declared Ellie. ''E'd look stupid appearing with no one to see 'im.'

We got back just in time for the funeral feast. It was a celebration of the first Earl's life and the centrepiece was Mrs Tiplady's Medenham Masterpiece. It was wonderful, and looked so real I thought it might crawl up the table and bow to the Queen at any moment!

Surely Her Majesty must have finished with Mr Secretary Cecil by now. There will scarcely be time for a masque if I do not leave these lazy bees and speak with her. I must run!

Afternoon, in the Long Gallery

It is about five of the clock and I have a busy night ahead. I am sitting by the portrait of the first Earl. The painting is no longer hidden away in a corner but has been hung with all ceremony on the other side of the fireplace to the one of the Queen. Her Majesty insisted. She told Lord Reynold that she would only come to view her portrait when his ancestor had been moved from the dingy corner. And of course Lord Reynold complied. The second Earl has been taken down without any ceremony at all, and stuck in the cupboard with the lady and the monkey. Lord Reynold declared he would not give wall space to murderers!

Anyway, when I left the orchard I went in search of the Queen. I found her just leaving her Privy Chamber. I charged up to her, fell to my knees and begged an audience. Her Majesty raised an eyebrow at my antics. Then she ushered me back into her Privy Chamber, waved away all the others and shut the door in their curious faces.

'You are in a fluster, Grace,' she said sternly. 'Some may think you disrespectful on this solemn day. What is amiss?'

'It is the ghost, Your Majesty,' I told her.

'But there is no ghost, my silly goddaughter,' snapped the Queen. 'You yourself told me he was merely an impostor.'

'Yes, and I know who that impostor is,' I said urgently. 'He is a former master builder of Lord Reynold's who bears him a grudge.' I told her all about George Colt and my evidence against him without saying how I had come upon it. I did not want to risk her wrath by telling her I had been in his house with only Ellie to protect me!

'Ever the Lady Pursuivant!' sighed the Queen with a smile. 'Why do you not let this matter rest? The first Earl has been buried. The so-called haunting will cease.'

'I fear Mr Colt may do something worse, Your Majesty,' I said earnestly. 'I now know that he is a sly and slippery character. I have no doubt that he will continue to cause mischief for Lord Reynold until he has humiliated him and shattered all his dreams.'

'That is serious indeed,' said the Queen. 'And he must be arrested. But we need evidence, Grace.'

I took a deep breath. 'I have a plan to trap him,' I said in a rush. 'I have told . . . I mean, I have let it be known to him that there is to be a masque tonight in the Rose Garden, where the ghost has been seen. I have had it put into his head that if the ghost of the old Earl appears, despite his body being laid to rest, then there is no hope for Medenham Manor. The builders will never return and the Court will leave. I thought he would not be able to resist putting in a ghostly appearance with so much at stake. And then the Gentlemen of the Guard will be able to arrest him and expose him for the impostor he is! There is but one flaw in my stratagem: there is no masque planned for tonight . . .' I fell silent and waited. I hardly dared look at the Queen. What would she think of my audacity?

To my great relief she threw back her head and laughed heartily. 'My dear Lady Pursuivant,' she said, taking my hands, 'you serve me well and bring me great joy into the bargain. There is only one course of action. I will command a masque for tonight.'

The Queen is truly the most magnificent person in the whole wide world.

As soon as I had thanked her and taken my leave, I hastened away to find Masou. I had to tell him the real reason for the masque.

Of course, because I was so anxious to find Masou, he proved hard to track down. It must have been a full half-hour before I found Mr Somers and his troupe in a small courtyard between the dairy and the bakehouse. Mr Somers was sorting through a pile of silks, and the tumblers were stretching their limbs in preparation for a practice. I could hear some discontented muttering going on. News of the masque must have reached them already!

'How now, Lady Grace,' called Mr Somers with an elaborate bow. 'Have you come with another request from Her Majesty? Does she wish us to fly to the moon? She has but to ask and we shall grow wings.'

Poor Mr Somers. I felt guilty that he must put on a performance at such short notice. But I needed to have a private word with Masou, so I offered to help with the costumes.

'I cannot think of letting you do such a thing, Lady Grace!' exclaimed Mr Somers. 'If Her Majesty should hear of it she will have me thrown in the dungeon!'

'I will not tell the Queen,' I said pleadingly.

'Very well!' he sighed with a mock tragic air. 'It matters not. It seems I must prepare myself to meet the rats one way or another. For if the masque is not ready she will throw me in there anyway!'

I scuttled off before he could change his mind. I sewed some beads onto a veil for French Louis, stuck feathers in a cap for little Gypsy Pete, and then made my way over to Masou with a length of white silk.

'We are all in a bother here, Grace,' he grumbled, as I draped the silk about him and started pinning it for a costume. 'First we pack our trunks on the Queen's orders, then we are to bide on the Queen's orders. Now we are to perform a masque at a moment's notice on the Queen's orders!'

'It's all my fault,' I admitted. I told Masou about Mr Colt and the trap I had set for him.

'You are a meddling Maid!' said Masou, pretending to be angry. Then he grinned. 'In truth you have done me a favour. I was growing tired of merely practising all day. We already have a masque prepared for Kenilworth, so we will do as much of it as we can.'

He suddenly wriggled in excitement and I nearly stuck a pin in him by mistake! 'Grace!' he exclaimed. 'I have a surprise for the masque. I would not spoil it for you by telling you what it is, but keep your eyes open tonight and not only for ghosts!'

'What are you planning?' I demanded.

But Masou merely winked annoyingly at me. I could have stuck a pin in him deliberately then, but I didn't.

I left the tumblers to their practice, wondering what Masou had planned. Then I retrieved my daybooke from my chamber and made my way here to the gallery. So the trap is set. I just have to hope that Mr Colt will take the bait. I would that I had some of Ellie's amulets. Then I could wish the venture good luck, for I fear we shall need it.

Hell's teeth! Yet again I cannot write in my bedchamber! Now there is no more talk of ghosts, but neither Mary Shelton nor Lady Sarah will put up with my candle while they are trying to sleep – even though they promised! I have had to seek refuge on a window ledge in the Musket Tower. Lord Reynold's new tower may look very grand but it has not a comfortable seat in it! Fie upon Mary Shelton and Lady Sarah! I shall have a sore bum because of them! However, I have too much to write to waste any more ink on them. So much has happened . . .

As the sun went down we followed Her Majesty out to the Rose Garden, where seats had been set out for the masque. I have to admit that I was very nervous as I sat down to wait next to the Queen. My stomach felt as if it were full of butterflies and they were all flying around at once! What if George Colt decided not to appear? I would have wasted everybody's time and Her Majesty might have something to say about that!

We were sitting facing the moat and the east wing, just where the oriel window jutted out. Mr Somers's troupe had done well in the little time they had been given. They had draped the walls of the old building in rich green cloth, to depict lush land beyond the water, and they had hung more cloth from the roof above. This was midnight blue and studded with silver and golden stars, to represent the sky. The whole scene was lit with hundreds of torches, and as the cloth gently swayed in the night air it appeared as if the stars were actually twinkling. A small stage had been erected on the narrow bank just in front of the oriel window. The scene was quite magical. Towering above, the ruin of the old east wing looked most mysterious against the darkening sky. It was indeed a dramatic place for a ghost to appear. I kept looking at the ledge above the oriel window, hoping the guards were keeping themselves well hidden.

Then Mr Somers stepped forward on the far bank and presented himself to the Queen and her Court with a deep bow. 'My Liege!' he cried, flinging out an arm for dramatic effect. 'My Lord and Lady of Medenham, members of the Court, we present to you a most tragical tale. It is a story of loyalty, heroism and bravery, and we dedicate it to the most noble, heroic and brave among us – our gracious and glorious Majesty!' He swept off his hat and made a deep bow as we all applauded. Every masque the troupe has ever performed has glorified Her Majesty in some way – and she never tires of the compliment. Poor Mr Somers must get a headache dreaming up new ideas to praise her!

Now other members of the troupe were appearing. Some, dressed in flowing green and brown costumes, took their places on either bank of the moat and began to sway rhythmically, as if they were reeds. Others, garbed in pale blue, moved among them playing the part of water nymphs.

'I shall tell the sorrowful tale of Hero,' Mr

Somers continued. 'This most beauteous and tender maiden lived long ago and far away in ancient Greece. She was priestess of Aphrodite, Goddess of Love.'

At this point a figure appeared at the oriel window, dressed in white voile and carrying a lantern. It was French Louis, who often seems to play the woman's part in our entertainments. He stepped out onto the little stage. It was lucky for him that the bottom bricks of the window had been taken away or he might have tripped in his long robes and gone straight into the moat! He was wearing the beaded veil that I had helped with and only his eyes could be seen. French Louis has a very dark beard and has to cover it well for each appearance.

'Hero loved a young man called Leander,' said our storyteller, 'and he returned her love.'

At that, Masou promptly sprang up right in front of us. He was dressed in his short white tunic with a belt, in the manner of the Greeks of long ago. He began to blow elaborate kisses over the water to Hero. French Louis sighed loudly and wrung his hands for all he was worth.

'Alas,' Mr Somers went on, 'the unhappy lovers were separated by the waters of the Hellespont, but true to his Hero, brave Leander swam across each night to be with her, guided by the light she shone for him.'

French Louis held up his lantern and Masou ran towards the moat, dived expertly into it and disappeared from view. This took some skill, for the Medenham moat is only deep in the middle. We could hear Masou swimming across to the other bank. Once there he reappeared, dripping wet, and swung himself up onto the platform in one graceful movement. The audience was very impressed, just as Masou intended, I am sure, and we all clapped. He came to the front of the platform and took several bows, only stopping when Mr Somers rather loudly and pointedly continued the story.

'At dawn, the lovers must needs part,' he said. A large wooden disc of bright gold rose from the bank next to them. It was mounted on a pole and was raised slowly up into the air. It wobbled a bit and I think it must have been Gypsy Pete holding it, for I could just see the top of a small hat with a feather. As soon as Leander saw the 'sun' he let out a horrified gasp, gave Hero a kiss on her cheek and disappeared inside the oriel window. Suddenly he appeared again, but this time running at full speed towards the moat. I thought he was about to dive into the water again, but no! Instead he launched himself off the stage and turned a double somersault high above the water!

There was a great gasp from the crowd as he flew through the air towards us. I could not believe that he could possibly land safely. I was sure he would crash into the side of the moat! But the next minute he had landed lightly on his feet, leaped up the bank and was taking endless bows in front of the Queen. Mr Somers was obviously as astonished as the rest of us and let him have his moment of glory. So that is what Masou had meant about a surprise!

I realized I had been so enthralled that I had not been watching out for the ghost at all! I quickly looked up at the ledge above the oriel window, but it was empty of spectres.

At last Will Somers took up the story again.

'One fateful night there was a storm. Yet faithful Leander would not fail his love. He plunged into the Hellespont and swam the rough waters.'

For a second time Masou dived into the moat and vanished from our sight. The human reeds on the banks made very realistic swishing noises and started to sway more and more violently as though caught in a storm.

'But alas,' went on Mr Somers, 'strong winds blew out Hero's lantern' – French Louis lifted up his veil a little and blew out his flame – 'and Leander had no light to guide him. He struggled bravely in the water, but could not reach the safety of the bank.'

We heard Masou splashing and shouting. Then suddenly he stopped. All was silent, but for the solemn voice of Mr Somers.

'Brave Leander drowned.'

The Queen rose quickly and walked to the edge of the moat to get a better view. The rest of us hurriedly followed her lead. We looked down at the dark waters below. A body floated there motionless and then slowly disappeared beneath the surface. It was Masou! I had to admire his acting skills (although I will not tell him so and make his head swell), for he truly looked dead. We waited for him to surface, but nothing happened. I confess I began to feel nervous for him. Clever though Masou is, I did not think that even he could stay under water for so long without drowning!

But at last there was a shout from the crowd – someone had spotted the body washed up on the bank, just under Hero's platform.

Hero set up a loud wailing and wrung her hands even more desperately than before. She began to tear her veil, but then stopped. I suppose French Louis remembered that he must keep his beard hidden!

'Our story ends in double woe!' Mr Somers finished with a flourish. 'As soon as she knew that her lover was dead, Hero, in despair, threw herself into the deep and cruel waters of the Hellespont.'

But before French Louis could get near the edge of the stage, there was a terrified scream from one of the Ladies-in-Waiting.

'The ghost is returned!'

The masque forgotten, we all looked up at the ledge of the oriel window, above the players. My plan had worked! There stood the ghost, pale in the moonlight, slowly raising a bony hand to point at us. Some of the ladies were crying out and fainting, and everyone drew back in fear. But unlike before, the ghost did not have time to vanish into the safety of the shadows. Two guards, with swords drawn, suddenly appeared and grasped him by the arms. The Court gasped in amazement as the ghost struggled with his captors. I breathed a sigh of relief: George Colt would be brought to justice at last!

'Upon my life I have never seen a ghost arrested before!' I heard someone next to me exclaim nervously.

'Silence!' ordered the Queen. 'It is plainly not a ghost at all!'

'Her Majesty is right,' said Mr Secretary Cecil. 'He looks solid enough now he has been apprehended!'

'Mayhap Mr Hatton's men have been granted special powers in these matters,' whispered the person next to me, 'for I warrant the apparition is indeed from beyond the grave.'

At that moment the ghost let out a very earthly cry and pulled free of the guards' grasp! He looked round wildly for a means of escape, but there was only one. After a brief moment of hesitation, he ran forward and threw himself over the low wall, plunging into the deep waters in the middle of the moat!

Mr Hatton barked an order and four guards ran along the bank. They tried to keep up with the fugitive but he easily outstripped them, helped by the flow of the water. He was heading for the river, and I feared that Mr Colt was going to get away!

Then, suddenly, the swimming figure disappeared under the surface as if he had been pulled down from below. The water churned madly and he appeared again, struggling with someone else in the waters of the moat! It was Masou! I realized that my friend must have swum after the impostor to block his escape. He grasped the ghost's arm and pulled him towards the bank and the waiting guards. I wanted to cheer; Masou was going to save the day!

But then George Colt caught Masou by the hair and wrenched his head back savagely. Masou cried out in pain and lost his grip on the villain's arm. The moat was shallower here, and Mr Colt must have got a firm foothold for he towered over Masou, who was now floundering desperately. I ran along towards them but there was nothing I could do. To my horror, Mr Colt forced Masou down under the water and held him there!

'Save him!' I shrieked, looking around wildly. Yet I could see that the Gentlemen of the Guard could not possibly reach Masou in time.

But now there was another figure in the water. A girl in a shift was wading towards the ghost. She was small and slight and determined-looking, and she was carrying a large jug in her hand. I could not believe my eyes! Ellie was coming to the rescue. But she should have been in the laundry. How could she possibly have known that her friend was in such grave danger?

She waded up behind George Colt, raised the jug and smashed it down on top of his head. He let go of his victim and fell back, stunned.

I scanned the surface of the water for Masou but there was no sign of him. 'Ellie!' I yelled. 'Do something!'

But Ellie had already plunged her hands into the water, searching for Masou. A moment later she pulled him to the surface, coughing and spluttering. By this time two of the guards had jumped into the moat, arrested the culprit and dragged him to the side. Behind them came Ellie, towing Masou, who was spitting water as he staggered up the bank. I was so relieved I wanted to rush up and hug them both, but I knew I had to stand still and bite my tongue. I hoped no one had taken note of my shouts.

Her Majesty now commanded that the prisoner be brought before her. He was flanked by Mr Hatton and two rows of men. They were not going to let him escape a second time. They forced him to his knees.

The Queen looked disdainfully at him, her eyes flashing dangerously. 'So the ghost deigns to walk among us!' she snapped. 'You have terrified my Court and tried to bring shame upon my good host and his wife. How dare you call Lord Reynold a traitor, when the only treachery has been your own? What have you to say for yourself?'

'My Liege,' muttered Mr Colt gruffly, 'I was led to my folly through my foolish anger.' He raised his hands in supplication towards the Queen, and put on a very piteous expression. 'I have committed a most grave sin and I beg Your Majesty's forgiveness.'

I do not believe he was sorry at all for his misdeeds. He was just sorry that he had been caught!

The Queen was unmoved. 'Cease your foolish prattling, man!' she exclaimed. 'I will hear not another word of your feeble excuses, but I will mete out fitting punishment for your crime. You shall be put in the stocks at first light tomorrow and the good people of Medenham may do as they please with you! You seem to want to perform, and I believe this way you will give great sport to your fellow villagers.'

'And not before time!' came a shrill cry.

Ellie looked as if she was about to cheer, but caught my eye and thought better of it. We all watched as George Colt was led away to be guarded until dawn, when his punishment would begin. I have heard that sometimes those in the stocks are not just pelted with rotten fruit and vegetables. Anyone who is really angry might cast stones and rocks. I hoped Mr Colt did not meet with such a fate, even though he had tried to drown my dear friend.

Now the Queen turned to Ellie and Masou. Ellie still had the handle of the broken jug clasped firmly in her hand and Masou was covered in weed. The two of them must have been very smelly, for the Queen kept waving her fan in their direction.

'Such bravery in my service shall not go unrewarded,' she said gravely. 'For that I wish to observe due ceremony – and the bank of a moat is not the place.' She looked them up and down and smiled. 'You have much of the moat about you at this time,' she continued, 'and I would not wish to put Lady Celia in a bad humour by having you drip on her fine floors. You are both to come to the Great Hall tomorrow at nine.'

The Queen turned to our host. 'Now, Lord Reynold,' she said. 'Pray escort me to my chambers. I have had enough excitement for one evening.'

Lord Reynold did as he was bidden. The poor man was speechless at yet another twist in the tale of the Medenham Ghost!

Of course we all had to retire if the Queen did, but the Court was slow to follow. Everyone was gossiping and exclaiming about the events we had just witnessed. I managed to catch Ellie's eye and beckoned to her to follow me. She gave Masou a nudge and they squelched along behind me at a respectful distance. I led them away from the crowds towards the back of the house.

Once we were alone outside the north door, Masou gave Ellie a huge, wet hug.

'You saved my life, fair Ellie,' he said solemnly.

'What fortune that you were by the water, Ellie!' I gasped, trying to help her wring some of the moat out of her clothes. 'How did you come to be there?'

'I 'ad a notion that Masou would do that somersault thingy,' she told us, 'for 'e said 'e had something planned, and I 'adn't seen it the last time on account of being underneath when 'e did 'is practice in the Kitchen Garden! Well, I made up this tale that Medenham water was renowned for getting out strawberry juice. And, of course, old Fadget couldn't resist sending me off in the dark to get some, so I was able to spy on the masque – and all along Mrs Fadget thought she was punishing me!'

'I never thought I would hear myself saying this,' said Masou, laughing, 'but I am most grateful to the old bat.'

I turned to him. 'But how did you stay under the water for so long when you were the drowning Leander?' I demanded. 'You gave me – I mean – some of the ladies of the Court cause for concern.'

'A trick of French Louis's,' explained Masou.

'And I wish I had been able to use it when Mr Colt held me under. I sank below the surface, turned onto my back and breathed through a reed. No one could see it in the darkness.'

'Just tell me beforehand in future!' I growled.

And now I will return to my bedchamber and try to sleep. It has all been so exciting that I fear I will have trouble. How strange that what started as a ghost story became a proper mystery for me to solve after all. I am greatly relieved that Mr Colt has been brought to justice and that nothing will now stop Lord Reynold finishing his new manor.

A few minutes later

Something very odd has just happened. I am still in the Musket Tower, for I had just closed my daybooke and was about to descend the stairs when I happened to glance out of the window. Down in the main courtyard I saw the figure of a man. I could not make out his garb except that he had a loose hat that hung in a point on his shoulder. The figure looked up and raised an arm, as if bidding me farewell. I blinked and rubbed my eyes and when I looked again, the courtyard was empty!

It was probably a trick of the moonlight.

Or was it the ghost of the first Earl, leaving the manor now that his bones have been laid to rest? One thing is for certain: he wore no ruff!

The Ninth Day of July, in the Year of Our Lord 1570

In my bedchamber

I am so excited that I can hardly hold my quill! My writing will look as if a monkey has done it but I do not care. The best thing ever has happened and this is the first time I have been able to take up my daybooke and write. It is already the afternoon.

At nine this morning the whole Court gathered in the Great Hall. Masou and Ellie came before Her Majesty, as she had commanded, and knelt down, looking very nervous.

'You have both served me well and loyally,' announced the Queen, 'and deserve reward for your actions last night.'

Ellie went as red as a radish. I wondered how she must feel to have all those people looking at her, when usually she is collecting laundry and completely ignored!

'Masou al-Ahmed,' said the Queen solemnly, 'such heroic deeds — and acrobatic feats — as you displayed last night deserve more than the title of tumbler. From henceforth you will be one of my Court Fools.'

Masou's face burst into a huge grin. 'Oh, Gracious Majesty,' he cried. 'You do me the most immense honour. It is . . . It is . . .'

I could not believe it. For the first time since I had met him, Masou was lost for words! I understood his bewilderment. He must have been overcome with joy! Being a Court Fool is a prestigious honour and will give Masou a pension too. It is no more than he deserves, and I am sure he will find his tongue when we are alone and tell me just that!

Then the Queen turned to Ellie. 'Ellie Bunting,' she said. Ellie seemed overcome by the honour of actually being addressed by Her Majesty, and tried to kneel down even further so that her nose was touching the floor. I think the Queen was aware of Ellie's discomfort for she went quickly on. 'You showed much courage in saving my new Fool and facing up to a devious enemy. It is clear to me that you are trustworthy and steadfast. One of my Maids of Honour is in great need of such a servant, so from this moment you are to leave the laundry and become tiring woman to Lady Grace Cavendish.'

Ellie gave such a gasp. She even dared to raise her head and look at the Queen in disbelief. My heart was thumping so fast I thought I would burst, and I had to stop myself from whooping with delight!

'I do not jest.' Her Majesty smiled. 'You will serve me well, for I am growing weary of that young lady appearing with her sleeves half tied. I warn you, it is an onerous duty! Now, I must ask one more thing of you, Ellie Bunting.' And the Queen broke off her speech and, to the amazement of everyone, gave Ellie a slow wink! 'No more breaking jugs over people's heads!' she chuckled.

Ellie gazed at the Queen in wonder. 'Oh, Your Majesty,' she sighed. 'I will . . . I mean, I won't . . . I mean . . .' And then she gave up trying to speak and kissed the hem of the Queen's skirts instead.

I stood there in the crowd of people trying to behave as a Maid of Honour should. And all the while I wanted to leap in the air and shout for joy and turn somersaults. I believe I was so happy that I could have jumped over the moat like Masou! But as I could not do that, I grabbed Mary Shelton's hand instead and squeezed it. She squeezed back. I knew she was pleased that I had a tiring woman of my own and I know she is fond of Ellie too.

Then Lord Reynold came forward to speak to Ellie and Masou. 'You will probably never know how much you have served me and my family,' he said, his voice breaking with emotion. And, without another word, he thrust a small purse of coins at each of them.

The Queen dismissed Masou and Ellie and they bowed out of the room. I craned round Mary Shelton to see them leave. When they reached the door, they clasped each other's hands and began to run in the direction of the main courtyard. I longed to be with them.

And at that moment I knew that Her Gracious Majesty, Queen Elizabeth, is so wonderful that she can even read minds, for, all of a sudden, she turned to me and fixed me with a stern look.

'Lady Grace Cavendish,' she commanded, 'I bid you walk my dogs this very minute, for they will grow fat. They need to be outside. They need to be in the *courtyard* this instant.' I understood her meaning and began to curtsy. 'Do not dawdle, girl,' she shouted. 'Get you gone!'

I went!

I ran along the passage and out into the main courtyard. I could see Masou and Ellie. They were dancing and skipping on the flagstones. They hadn't seen me yet and I hesitated in the doorway, drinking in the sight of their joyfulness.

'Queen's Fool!' Masou laughed. He let go of Ellie's hands and cartwheeled across the bridge and onto the grass beyond.

'No more Mrs Fadget!' squealed Ellie, running after him. 'And I'll be with Grace and no pretence needed.'

'And a purse of coins!' shouted Masou to the sky.

'I will have a new dress,' announced Ellie. 'Brand new, with no holes.'

For a moment I felt tears pricking at my eyes. No one in the whole world could have such true friends as I.

Then Ellie saw me. 'Grace!' she squealed, waving madly at me. 'Over here.'

I gave my eyes a hard rub and ran to join them. We all clasped hands and Masou pulled us round faster and faster in a giddy reel. Then we collapsed laughing on the grass.

This is the happiest day of my life!

GLOSSARY

amulet – an object, thought to be charmed, and believed to protect the wearer from evil

Bedlam – the major asylum for the insane in London during Elizabethan times – the name came from Bethlem Hospital

bodice – the top part of a woman's dress

bombast – cotton padding

brocade – a rich, gold-embroidered fabric

bum – bottom

carcanet – a jewelled necklace fitting closely around the neck like a choker

chemise – a loose shirt-like undergarment

daybooke – a book in which you would record your sins each day so that you could pray about them. The idea of keeping a diary or journal grew out of this. Grace is using hers as a journal

doublet – a close-fitting padded jacket worn by men

elf-shot – any small, triangular-shaped stone found in a field was said to have been made by the elves or fairies and was believed to bring good luck to the owner

evil eye – a term generally used to mean evil

flying buttress – a masonry structure designed to support a roof or wall

forepart – the part of the garment that covers the chest

gargoyle – a spout from a gutter, made in the shape of a human or animal figure, designed to throw rainwater away from a building

humours – the fluids of the body which were thought to control health and temperament

jerkin – a close-fitting, hip-length, usually sleeveless jacket

kirtle – the skirt section of an Elizabethan dress

Knot Garden – a formal garden made of bushes of flowers or herbs grown in geometric shapes to form a pattern

Lady-in-Waiting – one of the ladies who helped to look after the Queen and who kept her company

lead – lead carbonate, used for make-up

leche – a sweet, sugary substance

Lord Lieutenant – official responsible for managing local military affairs

Madeira – a sherry-like white wine from Madeira

Maid of Honour – a younger girl who helped to look after the Queen like a Lady-in-Waiting

Mary Shelton – one of Queen Elizabeth's Maids of Honour (a Maid of Honour of this name really did exist, see below). Most Maids of Honour were not officially 'ladies' (like Lady Grace) but they had to be of born of gentry

masque – a masquerade, a masked ball

mead – an alcoholic drink made with honey

megrim – a migraine headache

mullioned glass – small pieces of glass held together by strips of lead to form a window

mumming – acting

palliasse – a thin mattress

penner – a small leather case which would attach to a belt. It was used for holding quills, ink, knife and any other equipment needed for writing

physic – the art of medicine and healing

plague – a virulent disease which killed thousands

posset – a hot drink made from sweetened and spiced milk curdled with ale or wine

Presence Chamber – the room where Queen Elizabeth received people

on progress – term used when the Queen was touring parts of her realm. It was a kind of summer holiday for her

pursuivant – one who pursues someone else

Queen's favour – an item of the Queen's, worn to show that she favoured the wearer to win the contest

Queen's Guard – these were more commonly known as the Gentlemen Pensioners – young noblemen who guarded the Queen from physical attacks

Secretary Cecil – William Cecil, an administrator for the Queen (was later made Lord Burghley)

Shaitan – the Islamic word for Satan, though it means a trickster and a liar rather than the ultimate evil

stays – the boned, laced bodice worn around the body under the clothes. Victorians called it a corset

sweetmeats – sweets

Tilting Yard – area where knights in armour would joust or 'tilt' (i.e. ride at each other on horseback with lances)

tiring woman – a woman who helped a lady to dress

trencher – a wooden platter

tumbler – acrobat

In 1485 Queen Elizabeth I's grandfather, Henry Tudor, won the battle of Bosworth Field against Richard III and took the throne of England. He was known as Henry VII. He had two sons, Arthur and Henry. Arthur died while still a boy, so when Henry VII died in 1509, Elizabeth's father came to the throne and England got an eighth king called Henry – the notorious one who had six wives.

Wife number one – Catherine of Aragon – gave Henry one daughter called Mary (who was brought up as a Catholic), but no living sons. To Henry VIII this was a disaster, because nobody believed a queen could ever govern England. He needed a male heir.

Henry wanted to divorce Catherine so he could marry his pregnant mistress, Anne Boleyn. The Pope, the head of the Catholic Church, wouldn't allow him to annul his marriage, so Henry broke with the Catholic Church and set up the Protestant Church of England – or the Episcopal Church, as it's known in the USA.

Wife number two – Anne Boleyn – gave Henry another daughter, Elizabeth (who was brought up as a Protestant). When Anne then miscarried a baby boy, Henry decided he'd better get somebody new, so he accused Anne of infidelity and had her executed.

Wife number three – Jane Seymour – gave Henry a son called Edward, and died of childbed fever a couple of weeks later.

Wife number four – Anne of Cleves – had no children. It was a diplomatic marriage and Henry didn't fancy her, so she agreed to a divorce (wouldn't you?).

Wife number five – Catherine Howard – had no children either. Like Anne Boleyn, she was accused of infidelity and executed.

Wife number six – Catherine Parr – also had no children. She did manage to outlive Henry, though, but only by the skin of her teeth. Nice guy, eh?

Henry VIII died in 1547, and in accordance with the rules of primogeniture (whereby the first-born son inherits from his father), the person who succeeded him was the boy Edward. He became Edward VI. He was strongly Protestant, but died young in 1553.

Next came Catherine of Aragon's daughter, Mary, who became Mary I, known as Bloody Mary. She was strongly Catholic, married Philip II of Spain in a diplomatic match, but died childless five years later. She also burned a lot of Protestants for the good of their souls.

Finally, in 1558, Elizabeth came to the throne. She reigned until her death in 1603. She played the marriage game — that is, she kept a lot of important and influential men hanging on in hopes of marrying her — for a long time. At one time it looked as if she would marry her favourite, Robert Dudley, Earl of Leicester. She didn't though, and I think she probably never intended to get married — would you, if you'd had a dad like hers? So she never had any children.

She was an extraordinary and brilliant woman, and during her reign, England first started to become important as a world power. Sir Francis Drake sailed around the world —

raiding the Spanish colonies of South America for loot as he went. And one of Elizabeth's favourite courtiers, Sir Walter Raleigh, tried to plant the first English colony in North America – at the site of Roanoke in 1585. It failed, but the idea stuck.

The Spanish King Philip II tried to conquer England in 1588. He sent a huge fleet of 150 ships, known as the Invincible Armada, to do it. It failed miserably – defeated by Drake at the head of the English fleet – and most of the ships were wrecked trying to sail home. There were many other great Elizabethans, too – including William Shakespeare and Christopher Marlowe.

After her death, Elizabeth was succeeded by James VI of Scotland, who became James I of England and Scotland. He was almost the last eligible person available! He was the son of Mary Queen of Scots, who was Elizabeth's cousin, via Henry VIII's sister.

His son was Charles I – the King who was beheaded after losing the English Civil War.

★   ★   ★

The stories about Lady Grace Cavendish are set in the years 1569 and 1570, when Elizabeth was thirty-six and still playing the marriage game for all she was worth. The Ladies-in-Waiting and Maids of Honour at her Court weren't servants – they were companions and friends, supplied from upper-class families. Not all of them were officially 'ladies' – only those with titled husbands or fathers; in fact, many of them were unmarried younger daughters sent to Court to find themselves a nice rich lord to marry.

All the Lady Grace Mysteries are invented, but some of the characters in the stories are real people – Queen Elizabeth herself, of course, and Mrs Champernowne and Mary Shelton as well. There never was a Lady Grace Cavendish (as far as we know!) – but there were plenty of girls like her at Elizabeth's Court. The real Mary Shelton foolishly made fun of the Queen herself on one occasion – and got slapped in the face by Elizabeth for her trouble! But most of the time, the Queen seems to have been protective and kind to her Maids of Honour. She was very strict about boyfriends, though. There was one simple rule for boyfriends in those days: you couldn't have one. No boyfriends at all. You would get married to a person your parents chose for you and that was that. Of course, the girls often had other ideas!

Later on in her reign, the Queen had a full-scale secret service run by her great spymaster, Sir Francis Walsingham. His men, who hunted down priests and assassins, were called 'pursuivants'. There are also tantalizing hints that Elizabeth may have had her own personal sources of information – she certainly was very well informed, even when her counsellors tried to keep her in the dark. And who knows whom she might have recruited to find things out for her? There may even have been a Lady Grace Cavendish, after all!

A note on Elizabethan ghosts

In Elizabethan times most people believed in ghosts. Shakespeare included ghosts in several of his plays because he knew that many in his audience would believe in restless spirits – and be terrified!

Some ghosts were thought to be out for revenge and would come back to haunt their murderer, while some were the spectres of people who had behaved wrongly and whose spirits were doomed to walk the earth in punishment. Phantoms were said to appear in times of great change or to warn of something terrible coming (as if seeing a ghost wasn't bad enough!).

There were ways of protecting yourself from ghosts. You could carry amulets like Ellie's to ward off evil spirits, or say a prayer and make the sign of the cross on your forehead if you came across one.

One particularly famous ghost – and almost certainly the most famous at the time of our story – is that of Queen Elizabeth's own mother, Anne Boleyn. King Henry VIII had her beheaded in 1536, when Elizabeth was only two. And it was actually Henry VIII who was the first to see her ghost walking at

Hampton Court Palace. Perhaps she was back for revenge!

But Anne Boleyn did not stick to Hampton Court. Lady Grace might well have seen Anne's ghost at the Tower of London – now considered one of the most haunted sites in England. It was an obvious place for Anne to haunt, for it was there that she was executed.

People still claim to see the ghost of Anne Boleyn today. As well as haunting the Tower and Hampton Court she is said to return to her old home at Hever Castle in the county of Kent. Every Christmas Eve she wafts across the bridge which crosses the river in the castle grounds.

But perhaps her most dramatic appearance is in Norfolk. According to legend, every year on the nineteenth of May, the anniversary of her execution, Anne Boleyn arrives at Blickling Hall in a ghostly coach, carrying her severed head upon her lap. This is very clever of her, and we don't know where she finds the coach, for there were none when Anne was alive!

Interestingly, the ghost of Queen Elizabeth I

herself has been known to walk! Even though the Queen died peacefully at Richmond Palace, many people claim to have seen her, dressed all in black, walking through the Royal Library at Windsor Castle.

THE LADY GRACE MYSTERIES
EXILE

By Grace Cavendish

MAGIC AND MAYHEM!

There's a new arrival at Court. Banoo
Yasmine has a pet panther and is rumoured
to have magical powers. Yasmine also owns
the renowned Heart of Kings ruby. When
the famed jewel goes missing, the finger is
pointed at one of Grace's friends.
Can Grace find the true thief?

Lose yourself in the fascinating life of Court
in the daybooke of Lady Grace.

DOUBLEDAY
0 385 60850 0

THE LADY GRACE MYSTERIES
FEUD

By Grace Cavendish

POISONOUS PLOTS!

The Queen's portrait painters are at court,
bearing exotic colours with deadly
ingredients. Lady Grace is fascinated by the
work of the artists, especially when she
begins to suspect there is a poisoner at
work. Could the paints – or one of the
painters – be to blame?

Piece together the courtly clues within
the daybooke of Lady Grace.

DOUBLEDAY
0 385 60851 9